D1400091

A WHITE HERON

AND OTHER STORIES

SARAH ORNE JEWETT

Solis Press

To my dear sister Mary

First published in 1886. This edition published by Solis Press, 2013

Typographical arrangement copyright © Solis Press 2013

All rights reserved. No part of this publication may be reproduced, stored in a retrieval system, or transmitted, in any form or by any means, electronic, mechanical, photocopying, recording or otherwise, except as permitted by the UK Copyright, Designs and Patents Act 1988, without the prior permission of the publisher.

This book is sold subject to the condition that it shall not, by way or trade or otherwise, be lent, resold, hired out or otherwise circulated without the publisher's prior consent in any form of binding or cover other than in which it is published and without a similar condition including this condition being imposed on the subsequent purchaser.

ISBN: 978-1-907947-73-5

Published by Solis Press, PO Box 482, Tunbridge Wells TN2 9QT, Kent, England

Web: www.solispress.com | *Twitter*: @SolisPress

❧ CONTENTS ❧

Sarah Orne Jewett 1849–1909

❧ A WHITE HERON ❧

Part I.

THE WOODS WERE ALREADY filled with shadows one June evening, just before eight o'clock, though a bright sunset still glimmered faintly among the trunks of the trees. A little girl was driving home her cow, a plodding, dilatory, provoking creature in her behavior, but a valued companion for all that. They were going away from whatever light there was, and striking deep into the woods, but their feet were familiar with the path, and it was no matter whether their eyes could see it or not.

There was hardly a night the summer through when the old cow could be found waiting at the pasture bars; on the contrary, it was her greatest pleasure to hide herself away among the huckleberry bushes, and though she wore a loud bell she had made the discovery that if one stood perfectly still it would not ring. So Sylvia had to hunt for her until she found her, and call Co'! Co'! with never an answering Moo, until her childish patience was quite spent. If the creature had not given good milk and plenty of it, the case would have seemed very different to her owners. Besides, Sylvia had all the time there was, and very little use to make of it. Sometimes in pleasant weather it was a consolation to look upon the cow's pranks as an intelligent attempt to play hide and seek, and as the child had no playmates she lent herself to this amusement with a good deal of zest. Though this chase had been so long that the wary animal herself had given an unusual signal of her whereabouts, Sylvia had only laughed when she came upon Mistress Moolly at the swampside, and urged her affectionately homeward with a twig of birch leaves, The old cow was not inclined to wander farther, she even turned in the right direction for once as they left the pasture, and stepped along the road at a good pace. She was quite ready to be milked now, and seldom stopped to browse. Sylvia wondered what her grandmother would say because they were so late. It was a great while since she had left home at half-past five o'clock, but everybody knew the difficulty of making this errand a short one. Mrs. Tilley had chased the horned torment too many summer evenings herself to blame anyone else for lingering, and was only thankful as she waited that she had Sylvia, nowadays, to give such valuable assistance. The good woman suspected that Sylvia-loitered occasionally on her own account; there never was such a child for straying about out-of-doors since the world was made! Everybody said that it was a good change for a little maid who had tried to grow for eight years in a crowded manufacturing town, but, as for Sylvia herself, it seemed as if she never had been alive at all before she came to live at the farm. She thought often with wistful compassion of a wretched geranium that belonged to a town neighbor.

"'Afraid of folks,'" old Mrs. Tilley said to herself, with a smile, after she had made the unlikely choice of Sylvia from her daughter's houseful of children, and was returning to the farm. "'Afraid of folks,' they said! I guess she won't be troubled no great with 'em up to the old place!" When they reached the door of the lonely house and stopped to unlock it, and the cat came to purr loudly, and rub against them, a deserted pussy, indeed, but fat with young robins, Sylvia whispered that this was a beautiful place to live in, and she never should wish to go home.

<hr/>

The companions followed the shady wood-road, the cow taking slow steps and the child very fast ones. The cow stopped long at the brook to drink, as if the pasture were not half a swamp, and Sylvia stood still and waited, letting her bare feet cool themselves in the shoal water, while the great twilight moths struck softly against her. She waded on through the brook as the cow moved away, and listened to the thrushes with a heart that beat fast with pleasure. There was a stirring in the great boughs overhead. They were full of little birds and beasts that seemed to be wide awake, and going about their world, or else saying good-night to each other in sleepy twitters. Sylvia herself felt sleepy as she walked along. However, it was not much farther to the house, and the air was soft and sweet. She was not often in the woods so late as this, and it made her feel as if she were a part of the gray shadows and the moving leaves. She was just thinking how long it seemed since she first came to the farm a year ago, and wondering if everything went on in the noisy town just the same as when she was there the thought of the great red-faced boy who used to chase and frighten her made her hurry along the path to escape from the shadow of the trees.

Suddenly this little woods-girl is horror-stricken to hear, a clear whistle not very far away. Not a bird's-whistle, which would have a sort of friendliness, but a boy's whistle, determined, and somewhat aggressive. Sylvia via left the cow to whatever sad fate might await her, and stepped discreetly aside into the bushes, but she was just too late. The enemy had discovered her, and called out in a very cheerful and persuasive tone, "Halloa, little girl, how far is it to the road?" and trembling Sylvia answered almost inaudibly, "A good ways."

She did not dare to look boldly at the tall young man, who carried a gun over his shoulder, but she came out of her bush and again followed the cow, while he walked alongside.

I have been hunting for some birds," the stranger said kindly, "and I have lost my way, and need a friend very much. Don't be afraid," he added gallantly. "Speak up and tell me what your name is, and whether you think I can spend the night at your house, and go out gunning early in the morning."

Sylvia was more alarmed than before. Would not her grandmother consider her much to blame? But who could have foreseen such an accident as this? It did not seem to be her fault, and she hung her head as if the stem of it were broken, but managed to answer "Sylvy," with much effort when her companion again asked her name.

Mrs. Tilley was standing in the doorway when the trio came into view. The cow gave a loud moo by way of explanation.

"Yes, you'd better speak up for yourself, you old trial! Where'd she tucked herself away this time, Sylvy?" But Sylvia kept an awed silence; she knew by instinct that her grandmother did not comprehend the gravity of the situation. She must be mistaking the stranger for one of the farmer-lads of the region.

The young man stood his gun beside the door, and dropped a lumpy game-bag beside it; then he bade Mrs. Tilley good-evening, and repeated his wayfarer's story, and asked if he could have a night's lodging.

"Put me anywhere you like," he said. "I must be off early in the morning, before day; but I am very hungry, indeed. You can give me some milk at any rate, that's plain."

"Dear sakes, yes," responded the hostess, whose long slumbering hospitality seemed to be easily awakened. "You might fare better if you went out to the main road a mile or so, but you're welcome to what we've got. I'll milk right off, and you make yourself at home. You can sleep on husks or feathers," she proffered graciously. "I raised them all myself. There's good pasturing for geese just below here towards the ma'sh. Now step round and set a plate for the gentleman, Sylvy!" And Sylvia promptly stepped. She was glad to have something to do, and she was hungry herself.

It was a surprise to find so clean and comfortable a little dwelling in this New England wilderness. The young man had known the horrors of its most primitive housekeeping, and the dreary squalor of that level of society which does not rebel at the companionship of hens. This was the best thrift of an old-fashioned farmstead, though on such a small scale that it seemed like a hermitage. He listened eagerly to the old woman's quaint talk, he watched Sylvia's pale face and shining gray eyes with ever growing enthusiasm, and insisted that this was the best supper he had eaten for a month, and afterward the new-made friends sat down in the door-way together while the moon came up.

Soon it would be berry-time, and Sylvia was a great help at picking. The cow was a good milker, though a plaguey thing to keep track of, the hostess gossiped frankly, adding presently that she had buried four children, so Sylvia's mother, and a son (who might be dead) in California were all the children she had left. "Dan, my boy, was a great hand to go gunning," she explained sadly. "I never wanted for pa'tridges or gray squer'ls while he was to home. He's been a great wand'rer, I expect, and he's no hand to write letters. There, I don't blame him, I'd ha' seen the world myself if it had been so I could."

"Sylvy takes after him," the grandmother continued affectionately, after a minute's pause. "There ain't a foot o' ground she don't know her way over, and the wild creatures counts her one o' themselves. Squer'ls she'll tame to come an' feed right out o' her hands, and all sorts o' birds. Last winter she got the jaybirds to bangeing here, and I believe she'd 'a' scanted herself of her own meals to have plenty to throw out amongst 'em, if I hadn't kep' watch. Anything but crows, I tell her, I'm willin' to help support — though Dan he had a tamed one o' them that did seem to have reason same as folks. It was round here a good spell after he went away. Dan an' his father they didn't hitch, — but he never held up his head ag'in after Dan had dared him an' gone off."

The guest did not notice this hint of family sorrows in his eager interest in something else.

"So Sylvy knows all about birds, does she?" he exclaimed, as he looked round at the little girl who sat, very demure but increasingly sleepy, in the moonlight. "I am making a collection of birds myself. I have been at it ever since I was a boy." (Mrs. Tilley smiled.) "There are two or three very rare ones I have been hunting for these five years. I mean to get them on my own ground if they can be found."

"Do you cage 'em up?" asked Mrs. Tilley doubtfully, in response to this enthusiastic announcement.

"Oh no, they're stuffed and preserved, dozens and dozens of them," said the ornithologist, "and I have shot or snared every one myself. I caught a glimpse of a white heron a few miles from here on Saturday, and I have followed it in this direction. They have never been found in this district at all. The little white heron, it is," and he turned again to look at Sylvia with the hope of discovering that the rare bird was one of her acquaintances.

But Sylvia was watching a hop-toad in the narrow footpath.

"You would know the heron if you saw it," the stranger continued eagerly. "A queer tall white bird with soft feathers and long thin legs. And it would have a nest perhaps in the top of a high tree, made of sticks, something like a hawk's nest."

Sylvia's heart gave a wild beat; she knew that strange white bird, and had once stolen softly near where it stood in some bright green swamp grass, away over at the other side of the woods. There was an open place where the sunshine always seemed strangely yellow and hot, where tall, nodding rushes grew, and her grandmother had warned her that she might sink in the soft black mud underneath and never be heard of more. Not far beyond were the salt-marshes just this side the sea itself, which

Sylvia wondered and dreamed much about, but never had seen, whose great voice could sometimes be heard above the noise of the woods on stormy nights.

"I can't think of anything I should like so much as to find that heron's nest," the handsome stranger was saying. "I would give ten dollars to anybody who could show it to me," he added desperately, "and I mean to spend my whole vacation hunting for it if need be. Perhaps it was only migrating, or had been chased out of its own region by some bird of prey."

Mrs. Tilley gave amazed attention to all this but Sylvia still watched the toad, not divining as she might have done at some calmer time, that the creature wished to get to its hole under the door-step, and was much hindered by the unusual spectators at that hour of the evening. No amount of thought, that night, could decide how many wished-for treasures the ten dollars, so lightly spoken of, would buy.

The next day the young sportsman hovered about the woods, and Sylvia kept him company, having lost her first fear of the friendly lad, who proved to be most kind and sympathetic. He told her many things about the birds and what they knew and where they lived and what they did with themselves. And he gave her a jack-knife, which she thought as great a treasure as if she were a desert-islander. All day long he did not once make her troubled or afraid except when he brought down some unsuspecting singing creature from its bough. Sylvia would have liked him vastly better without his gun; she could not understand why he killed the very birds he seemed to like so much. But as the day waned, Sylvia still watched the young man with loving admiration. She had never seen anybody so charming and delightful; the woman's heart, asleep in the child, was vaguely thrilled by a dream of love. Some premonition of that great power stirred and swayed these young creatures who traversed the solemn woodlands with soft-footed silent care. They stopped to listen to a bird's song; they pressed forward again eagerly, parting the branches — speaking to each other rarely and in whispers; the young man going first and Sylvia following, fascinated, a few steps behind, with her gray eyes dark with excitement.

She grieved because the longed-for white heron was elusive, but she did not lead the guest, she only followed, and there was no such thing as speaking first. The sound of her own unquestioned voice would have terrified her — it was hard enough to answer yes or no when there was need of that. At last evening began to fall, and they drove the cow home together, and Sylvia smiled with pleasure when they came to the place where she heard the whistle and was afraid only the night before.

Part II.

Half a mile from home, at the farther edge of the woods, where the land was highest, a great pine-tree stood, the last of its generation. Whether it was left for a boundary mark, or for what reason, no one could say; the wood choppers who had felled its mates were dead and gone long ago, and a whole forest of sturdy trees, pines and oaks and maples, had grown again. But the stately head of this old pine towered above them all and made a land-mark for sea and shore miles and miles away. Sylvia knew it well. She had always believed that whoever climbed to the top of it could see the ocean; and the little girl had often laid her hand on the great rough trunk and looked up wistfully at those dark boughs that the wind always stirred, no matter how hot and still the air might be below. Now she thought of the tree with a new excitement, for why, if one climbed it at break of day could not one see all the world, and easily discover from whence the white heron flew, and mark the place, and find the hidden nest?

What a spirit of adventure, what wild ambition! What fancied triumph and delight and glory for the later morning when she could make known the secret! It was almost too real and too great for the childish heart to bear.

All night the door of the little house stood open and the whippoorwills came and sang upon the very step. The young sportsman and his old hostess were sound asleep, but Sylvia's great design kept her broad awake and watching. She forgot to think of sleep. The short summer night seemed as long as the winter darkness, and at last when the whippoorwills ceased, and she was afraid the morning would after all come too soon, she stole out of the house and followed the pasture path through the woods, hastening toward the open ground beyond, listening with a sense of comfort and companionship to the drowsy twitter of a half-awakened bird, whose perch she had jarred in passing. Alas, if the great wave of human interest which flooded for the first time this dull little life should sweep away the satisfactions of an existence heart to heart with nature and the dumb life of the forest!

There was the huge tree asleep yet in the paling moonlight, and small and silly Sylvia began with utmost bravery to mount to the top of it, with tingling, eager blood coursing the channels of her whole frame, with her bare feet and fingers, that pinched and held like bird's claws to the monstrous ladder reaching up, up, almost to the sky itself. First she must mount the white oak tree that grew alongside, where she was almost lost among the dark branches and the green leaves heavy and wet with dew; a bird fluttered off its nest, and a red squirrel ran to and fro and scolded pettishly at the harmless housebreaker. Sylvia felt her way easily. She had often climbed there, and knew that higher still one of the oak's upper branches chafed against the pine trunk, just where its lower boughs were set close together. There, when she made the dangerous pass from one tree to the other, the great enterprise would really begin.

She crept out along the swaying oak limb at last, and took the daring step across into the old pine-tree. The way was harder than she thought; she must reach far and hold fast, the sharp dry twigs caught and held her and scratched her like angry talons, the pitch made her thin little fingers clumsy and stiff as she went round and round the tree's great stem, higher and higher upward. The sparrows and robins in the woods below were beginning to wake and twitter to the dawn, yet it seemed much lighter there aloft in the pine-tree, and the child knew she must hurry if her project were to be of any use.

The tree seemed to lengthen itself out as she went up, and to reach farther and farther upward. It was like a great main-mast to the voyaging earth; it must truly have been amazed that morning through all its ponderous frame as it felt this determined spark of human spirit wending its way from higher branch to branch. Who knows how steadily the least twigs held themselves to advantage this light, weak creature on her way! The old pine must have loved his new dependent. More than all the hawks, and bats, and moths, and even the sweet voiced thrushes, was the brave, beating heart of the solitary gray-eyed child. And the tree stood still and frowned away the winds that June morning while the dawn grew bright in the east.

Sylvia's face was like a pale star, if one had seen it from the ground, when the last thorny bough was past, and she stood trembling and tired but wholly triumphant, high in the tree-top. Yes, there was the sea with the dawning sun making a golden dazzle over it, and toward that glorious east flew two hawks with slow-moving pinions. How low they looked in the air from that height when one had only seen them before far up, and dark against the blue sky. Their gray feathers were as soft as moths; they seemed only a little way from the tree, and Sylvia felt as if she too could go flying away among the clouds. Westward, the woodlands and farms reached miles and miles into the distance; here and there were church steeples, and white villages, truly it was a vast and awesome world!

The birds sang louder and louder. At last the sun came up bewilderingly bright. Sylvia could see the white sails of ships out at sea, and the clouds that were purple and rose-colored and yellow at first began to fade away. Where was the white heron's nest in the sea of green branches, and was this wonderful sight and pageant of the world the only reward for having climbed to such a giddy height? Now look down again, Sylvia, where the green marsh is set among the shining birches and dark hemlocks; there where you saw the white heron once you will see him again; look, look! a white spot of him like a single floating feather comes up from the dead hemlock and grows larger, and rises, and comes close at last, and goes by the land-mark pine with steady sweep of wing and outstretched slender neck and crested head. And wait! wait! do not move a foot or a finger, little girl, do not send an arrow of light and consciousness from your two eager eyes, for the heron has perched on a pine bough not far beyond yours, and cries back to his mate on the nest and plumes his feathers for the new day!

The child gives a long sigh a minute later when a company of shouting cat-birds comes also to the tree, and vexed by their fluttering and lawlessness the solemn heron goes away. She knows his secret now, the wild, light, slender bird that floats and wavers, and goes back like an arrow presently to his home in the green world beneath. Then Sylvia, well satisfied, makes her perilous way down again, not daring to look far below the branch she stands on, ready to cry sometimes because her fingers ache and her lamed feet slip. Wondering over and over again what the stranger would say to her, and what he would think when she told him how to find his way straight to the heron's nest.

⸎

"Sylvy, Sylvy!" called the busy old grandmother again and again, but nobody answered, and the small husk bed was empty and Sylvia had disappeared.

The guest waked from a dream, and remembering his day's pleasure hurried to dress himself that might it sooner begin. He was sure from the way the shy little girl looked once or twice yesterday that she had at least seen the white heron, and now she must really be made to tell. Here she comes now, paler than ever, and her worn old frock is torn and tattered, and smeared with pine pitch. The grandmother and the sportsman stand in the door together and question her, and the splendid moment has come to speak of the dead hemlock-tree by the green marsh.

But Sylvia does not speak after all, though the old grandmother fretfully rebukes her, and the young man's kind, appealing eyes are looking straight in her own. He can make them rich with money; he has promised it, and they are poor now. He is so well worth making happy, and he waits to hear the story she can tell.

No, she must keep silence! What is it that suddenly forbids her and makes her dumb? Has she been nine years growing and now, when the great world for the first time puts out a hand to her, must she thrust it aside for a bird's sake? The murmur of the pine's green branches is in her ears, she remembers how the white heron came flying through the golden air and how they watched the sea and the morning together, and Sylvia cannot speak; she cannot tell the heron's secret and give its life away.

⸎

Dear loyalty, that suffered a sharp pang as the guest went away disappointed later in the day, that could have served and followed him and loved him as a dog loves! Many a night Sylvia heard the echo of his whistle haunting the pasture path as she came home with the loitering cow. She forgot even her sorrow at the sharp report of his gun and the sight of thrushes and sparrows dropping silent to the ground, their songs hushed and their pretty feathers stained and wet with blood. Were the birds better friends than their hunter might have been, — who can tell? Whatever treasures were lost to her, woodlands and summer-time, remember! Bring your gifts and graces and tell your secrets to this lonely country child!

§ THE GRAY MAN §

HIGH ON THE SOUTHERN slope of Agamenticus there may still be seen the remnant of an old farm. Frost-shaken stone walls surround a fast-narrowing expanse of smooth turf which the forest is overgrowing on every side. The cellar is nearly filled up, never having been either wide or deep, and the fruit of a few mossy apple-trees drops ungathered to the ground. Along one side of the forsaken garden is a thicket of seedling cherry-trees to which the shouting robins come year after year in busy flights; the caterpillars' nests are unassailed and populous in this untended hedge. At night, perhaps, when summer twilights are late in drawing their brown curtain of dusk over the great rural scene, — at night an owl may sit in the hemlocks near by and hoot and shriek until the far echoes answer back again. As for the few men and women who pass this deserted spot, most will be repulsed by such loneliness, will even grow impatient with those mistaken fellow-beings who choose to live in solitude, away from neighbors and from schools, — yes, even from gossip and petty care of self or knowledge of the trivial fashions of a narrow life.

Now and then one looks out from this eyrie, across the wide-spread country, who turns to look at the sea or toward the shining foreheads of the mountains that guard the inland horizon, who will remember the place long afterward. A peaceful vision will come, full of rest and benediction into busy and troubled hours, to those who understand why some one came to live in this place so near the sky, so silent, so full of sweet air and woodland fragrance; so beaten and buffeted by winter storms and garlanded with summer greenery; where the birds are nearest neighbors and a clear spring the only wine-cellar, and trees of the forest a choir of singers who rejoice and sing aloud by day and night as the winds sweep over. Under the cherry thicket or at the edge of the woods you may find a stray-away blossom, some half-savage, slender grandchild of the old flower-plots, that you gather gladly to take away, and every year in June a red rose blooms toward which the wild pink roses and the pale sweet briars turn wondering faces as if a queen had shown her noble face suddenly at a peasant's festival.

There is everywhere a token of remembrance, of silence and secrecy. Some stronger nature once ruled these neglected trees and this fallow ground. They will wait the return of their master as long as roots can creep through mold, and the mold made way for them. The stories of strange lives have been whispered to the earth, their thoughts have burned themselves into the cold rocks. As one looks from the lower country toward the long slope of the great hillside, this old abiding-place marks the dark covering of trees like a scar. There is nothing to hide either the sunrise or the sunset. The low lands reach out of sight into the west and the sea fills all the east.

The first owner of the farm was a seafaring man who had through freak or fancy come ashore and cast himself upon the bounty of nature for support in his later years, though tradition keeps a suspicion of buried treasure and of a dark history. He cleared his land and built his house, but save the fact that he was a Scotsman no one knew to whom he belonged, and when he died the state inherited the unclaimed property. The only piece of woodland that was worth anything was sold and added to another farm, and the dwelling-place was left to the sunshine and the rain, to the birds that built their nests in the chimney or under the eaves. Sometimes a strolling company of country boys would find themselves near the house on a holiday afternoon, but the more dilapidated the small structure became, the more they believed that some uncanny existence possessed the lonely place, and the path that led toward the clearing at last became almost impassable.

Once a number of officers and men in the employ of the Coast Survey were encamped at the top of the mountain, and they smoothed the rough track that led down to the spring that bubbled from under a sheltering edge. One day a laughing fellow, not content with peering in at the small windows of the house, put his shoulder against the rain-blackened door and broke the simple fastening. He hardly knew that he was afraid as he first stood within the single spacious room, so complete a curiosity took possession of him. The place was clean and bare, the empty cupboard doors stood open, and yet the sound of his companions' voices outside seemed far away, and an awful sense that some unseen inhabitant followed his footsteps made him hurry out again pale and breathless to the fresh air and sunshine. Was this really a dwelling-place of spirits, as had been already hinted? The story grew more fearful, and spread quickly like a mist of terror among the lowland farms. For years the tale of the coast-surveyor's adventure in the haunted house was slowly magnified and told to strangers or to wide-eyed children by the dim firelight. The former owner was supposed to linger still about his old home, and was held accountable for deep offense in choosing for the scene of his unsuccessful husbandry a place that escaped the proprieties and restraints of life upon lower levels. His grave was concealed by the new growth of oaks and beeches, and many a lad and full-grown man beside has taken to his heels at the flicker of light from across a swamp or under a decaying tree in that neighborhood. As the world in some respects grew wiser, the good people near the mountain understood less and less the causes of these simple effects, and as they became familiar with the visible world, grew more shy of the unseen and more sensitive to unexplained foreboding.

One day a stranger was noticed in the town, as a stranger is sure to be who goes his way with quick, furtive steps straight through a small village or along a country road. This man was tall and had just passed middle age. He was well made and vigorous, but there was an unusual pallor in his face, a grayish look, as if he had been startled by bad news. His clothes were somewhat peculiar, as if they had been made in another country, yet they suited the chilly weather, being homespun of undyed wools, just the color of his hair, and only a little darker than his face or hands. Some one observed in one brief glance as he and this gray man met and passed each other, that his eyes bad a strange faded look; they might, however, flash and be coal-black in a moment of rage. Two or three persons stepped forward to watch the wayfarer as he went along the road with long, even strides, like one taking a journey on foot, but he quickly reached a turn of the way and was out of sight. They wondered who he was; one recalled some recent advertisement of an escaped criminal, and another the appearance of a native of the town who was supposed to be long ago lost at sea, but one surmiser knew as little as the next. If they had followed fast enough they might have tracked the mysterious man straight across the country, threading the by-ways, the shorter paths that led across the fields where the road was roundabout and hindering. At last he disappeared in the leafless, trackless woods that skirted the mountain.

That night there was for the first time in many years a twinkling light in the window of the haunted house, high on the hill's great shoulder; one farmer's wife and another looked up curiously, while they wondered what daring human being had chosen that awesome spot of all others for his home or for even a transient shelter. The sky was already heavy with snow; he might be a fugitive from justice, and the startled people looked to the fastening of their doors unwontedly that night, and waked often from a troubled sleep.

An instinctive curiosity and alarm possessed the country men and women for a while, but soon faded out and disappeared. The new-comer was by no means a hermit; he tried to be friendly, and inclined toward a certain kindliness and familiarity. He bought a comfortable store of winter provisions from his new acquaintances, giving every one his price, and spoke more at length, as time went on, of current events, of politics and the weather, and the town's own news and concerns. There was a sober cheerfulness about the man, as if he had known trouble and perplexity, and was fulfilling some mission that gave him pain; yet he saw some gain and reward beyond; therefore he could be contented with his life and such strange surroundings. He was more and more eager to form brotherly relations with the farmers near his home. There was almost a pleading look in his kind face at times, as if he feared the later prejudice of his associates. Surely this was no common or uneducated person, for in every way he left the stamp of his character and influence upon men and things. His reasonable words of advice and warning are current as sterling coins in that region yet; to one man he taught a new rotation of crops, to another he gave some priceless cures for devastating diseases of cattle. The lonely women of those remote country homes learned of him how to achieve their household toil with less labor and drudgery, and here and there he singled out promising children and kept watch of their growth, giving freely a most affectionate companionship, and a fair start in the journey of life. He taught those who were guardians of such children to recognize and further the true directions and purposes of existence; and the easily warped natures grew strong and well-established under his thoughtful care. No wonder that some people were filled with amazement, and thought his wisdom supernatural, from so many proofs that his horizon was wider than their own.

Perhaps some envious soul, or one aggrieved by being caught in treachery or deception, was the first to find fault with the stranger. The prejudice against his dwelling-place, and the superstition which had become linked to him in consequence, may have led back to the first suspicious attitude of the community. The whisper of distrust soon started on an evil way. If he were not a criminal, his past was surely a hidden one, and shocking to his remembrance, but the true foundation of all dislike was the fact that the gray man who went to and fro, living his simple, harmless life among them, *never was seen to smile*. Persons who remember him speak of this with a shudder, for nothing is more evident than that his peculiarity became at length intolerable to those whose minds lent themselves readily to suspicion. At first, blinded by the gentle good fellowship of the stranger, the changeless expression of his face was scarcely observed, but as the winter wore away he was watched with renewed disbelief and dismay.

After the first few attempts at gaiety nobody tried to tell a merry story in his presence. The most conspicuous of a joker's audience does a deep-rankling injustice if he sits with unconscious, un-amused face at the receipt of raillery. What a chilling moment when the gray man softly opened the door of a farmhouse kitchen, and seated himself like a skeleton at the feast of walnuts and roasted apples beside the glowing fire! The children whom he treated so lovingly, to whom he ever gave his best, though they were won at first by his gentleness, when they began to prattle and play with him would raise their innocent eyes to his face and hush their voices and creep away out of his sight. Once only he was bidden to a wedding, but never afterward, for a gloom was quickly spread through the boisterous company; the man who never smiled had no place at such a festival. The wedding guests looked over their shoulders again and again in strange foreboding, while he was in the house, and were burdened with a sense of coming woe for the newly-married pair. As one caught sight of his, among the faces of the rural folk, the gray man was like a somber mask, and at last the bridegroom flung open the door with a meaning gesture, and the stranger went out like a hunted creature, into the bitter coldness and silence of the winter night.

Through the long days of the next summer the outcast of the wedding, forbidden, at length, all the once-proffered hospitality, was hardly seen from one week's end to another's. He cultivated his poor estate with patient care, and the successive crops of his small garden, the fruits and berries of the wilderness, were food enough. He seemed unchangeable, and was always ready when he even guessed at a chance to be of use. If he were repulsed, he only turned away and went back to his solitary home. Those persons who by chance visited him there tell wonderful tales of the wild birds which had been tamed to come at his call and cluster about him, of the orderliness and delicacy of his simple life. The once-neglected house was covered with vines that he had brought from the woods, and planted about the splintering, decaying walls. There were three or four books in worn bindings on a shelf above the fire-place; one longs to know what volumes this mysterious exile had chosen to keep him company!

There may have been a deeper reason for the withdrawal of friendliness; there are vague rumors of the gray man's possession of strange powers. Some say that he was gifted with amazing strength, and once when some belated hunters found shelter at his fireside, they told eager listeners afterward that he did not sleep but sat by the fire reading gravely while they slumbered uneasily on his own bed of boughs. And in the dead of night an empty chair glided silently toward him across the floor as he softly turned his pages in the flickering light.

But such stories are too vague, and in that neighborhood too common to weigh against the true dignity and bravery of the man. At the beginning of the war of the rebellion he seemed strangely troubled and disturbed, and presently disappeared, leaving his house key with a neighbor as if for a few days' absence. He was last seen striding rapidly through the village a few miles away, going back along the road by which he had come a year or two before. No, not last seen either; for in one of the first battles of the war, as the smoke suddenly lifted, a farmer's boy, reared in the shadow of the mountain, opened his languid pain-dulled eyes as he lay among the wounded, and saw the gray man riding by on a tall horse. At that moment the poor lad thought in his faintness and fear that Death himself rode by in the gray man's likeness; unsmiling Death who tries to teach and serve mankind so that he may at the last win welcome as a faithful friend!

§ FARMER FINCH §

It was as bleak and sad a day as one could well imagine. The time of year was early in December, and the daylight was already fading, though it was only a little past the middle of the afternoon. John Finch was driving toward his farm, which he had left early in the morning to go to town; but to judge from his face one might have been sure that his business had not been successful. He looked pinched and discouraged with something besides the cold, and he hardly noticed the faithful red horse which carefully made its way over the frozen ruts of the familiar road.

There had lately been a few days of mild weather, when the ground had had time to thaw, but with a sudden blast of cold this deep mud had become like iron, rough and ragged, and jarring the people and horses cruelly who tried to travel over it. The road lay through the bleak country side of the salt-marshes which stretched themselves away toward the sea, dotted here and there with hay-cocks, and crossed in wavering lines by the inlets and ditches, filled now with grayish ice, that was sinking and cracking as the tide ran out. The marsh-grass was wind-swept and beaten until it looked as soft and brown as fur; the wind had free course over it, and it looked like a deserted bit of the world; the battered and dingy flat-bottomed boats were fastened securely in their tiny harbors, or pulled far ashore as if their usefulness was over, not only for that season but for all time. In some late autumn weather one feels as if summer were over with forever, and as if no resurrection could follow such unmistakable and hopeless death.

Where the land was higher it looked rocky and rough, and behind the marshes there were some low hills looking as if they were solid stone to their cores, and sparingly overgrown with black and rigid cedars. These stood erect from the least to the greatest, a most unbending and heartless family, which meant to give neither shade in summer nor shelter in winter. No wind could overturn them, for their roots went down like wires into the ledges, and no drought could dry away the inmost channels of vigorous though scanty sap that ran soberly through their tough, unfruitful branches.

In one place the hills formed an amphitheater open on the side toward the sea, and here on this bleak day it seemed as if some dismal ceremony were going forward. As one caught sight of the solemn audience of black and gloomy cedars that seemed to have come together to stand on the curving hillsides, one instinctively looked down at the level arena of marsh-land below, half fearing to see some awful sacrificial rite or silent combat. It might be an angry company of hamadryads who had taken the shape of cedar-trees on this day of revenge and terror. It was difficult to believe that one would ever see them again, and that the summer and winter days alike would find them looking down at the grave business which was invisible to the rest of the world. The little trees stood beside their elders in families, solemn and stern, and some miserable men may have heard the secret as they stumbled through the snow praying for shelter, lost and frozen on a winter night.

If you lie down along the rough grass in the slender shadow of a cedar and look off to sea, in a summer afternoon, you only hear a whisper like "Hush! hush!" as the wind comes through the stiff branches. The boughs reach straight upward; you cannot lie underneath and look through them at the sky; the tree all reaches away from the ground as if it had a horror of it, and shrank from even the breeze and the sunshine.

On this December day, as the blasts of wind struck them, they gave one stiff, unwilling bend, and then stood erect again. The road wound along between the sea-meadows and the hills, and poor John Finch seemed to be the only traveler. He was lost in thought, and the horse still went plodding on. The worn buffalo-robe was dragging from one side of the wagon, and had slipped down off the driver's knees. He hardly knew that he held the reins. He was in no hurry to get home, cold as it was, for he had only bad news to tell.

Polly Finch, his only daughter, was coming toward home from the opposite direction, and with her also things had gone wrong. She was a bright, good-natured girl of about twenty, but she looked old and care-worn that day. She was dressed in her best clothes, as if she had been away on some important affair, perhaps to a funeral, and she was shivering and wholly chilled in spite of the shawl which her mother had insisted upon her carrying. It had been a not uncomfortable morning for that time of year, and she had flouted the extra wrap at first, but now she hugged it close, and half buried her face in its folds. The sky was gray and heavy, except in the west, where it was a clear, cold shade of yellow. All the leafless bushes and fluffy brown tops of the dead asters and golden-rods stood out in exquisitely delicate silhouettes against the sky on the high road-sides, while some tattered bits of blackberry vine held still a dull glow of color. As Polly passed a barberry bush that grew above her she was forced to stop, for, gray and winterish as it had been on her approach, when she looked at it from the other side it seemed to be glowing with rubies. The sun was shining out pleasantly now that it had sunk below the clouds, and in these late golden rays the barberry bush had taken on a great splendor. It gave Polly a start, and it cheered her not a little, this sudden transformation, and she even went back along the road a little way to see it again as she had at first in its look of misery. The berries that still clung to its thorny branches looked dry and spoiled, but a few steps forward again made them shine out, and take on a beauty that neither summer nor autumn had given them, and Polly gave her head a little shake. "There are two ways of looking at more things than barberry bushes," she said, aloud, and went off with brisker steps down the road.

At home in the farmhouse Mrs. Finch had been waiting for her husband and daughter to come, until she had grown tired and hungry and almost frightened. Perhaps the day had been longer and harder to her than to anyone else. She had thought of so many cautions and suggestions that she might have given them both, and though the father's errand was a much more important one, still she had built much hope on the possibility of Polly's encounter with the school committee proving successful. Things had been growing very dark in Mr. Finch's business affairs, and they had all looked with great eagerness toward her securing a situation as teacher of one of the town schools. It was at no great distance, so that Polly could easily board at home, and many things seemed to depend upon it, even if the bank business turned out better than was feared. Our heroine had in her childhood been much praised for her good scholarship, and stood at the head of the district school, and it had been urged upon her father and mother by her teachers, and by other friends more or less wise, that she should have what they called an education. It had been a hard thing both for her father to find the money, and for her mother to get on without her help in the housework, but they had both managed to get along, and Polly had acquitted herself nobly in the ranks of a neighboring academy, and for the last year had been a pupil in the normal school. She had been very happy in her school life, and very popular both with scholars and teachers. She was friendly and social by nature, and it had been very pleasant to her to be among so many young people. The routine and petty ceremony of her years of study did not fret her, for she was too strong and good-natured even to be worn upon or much tired with the unwholesome life she lived. It was easy enough for her to get her lessons, and so she went through with flying colors, and cried a little when the last day arrived; but she felt less regret than most of the girls who were turned out then upon the world, some of them claiming truthfully that they had finished their education, since they had not wit enough to learn anything more, either with school-books in their hands or without them.

It came to Polly's mind as she stood in a row with the rest of the girls, while the old minister who was chief of the trustees gave them their diplomas, and some very good advice besides: "I wonder why we all made up our minds to be teachers? I wonder if we are going to be good ones, and if I shouldn't have liked something else a great deal better?"

Certainly she had met with a disappointment at the beginning of her own career, for she had seen that it was necessary for her to be within reach of home, and it seemed as if every school of the better class had been provided with a teacher. She had been so confident of her powers and mindful of her high standing at the normal school that it seemed at first that a fine position ought to be hers for the asking. But one after another her plans had fallen to the ground, until this last one, which had just been decided against her also. It had never occurred to her at first as a possible thing that she should apply for the small town school in her own district; to tell the truth, it was a great downfall of pride to the family, but they had said to each other that it would be well for Polly to have the winter at home, and in spring she could suit herself exactly. But everybody had felt the impossibility of her remaining idle, and no wonder her heart sank as she went toward home, knowing that she must tell them that another had been chosen to fill the place.

Mrs. Finch looked at the fire, and looked out of the window down the road, and took up the stocking she was knitting and tried to work at it; but every half-hour that went by doubled her uneasiness, and she looked out of the window altogether at last, until the fire was almost burned out, and the knitting lay untouched in her lap. She was a tall, fine looking woman, with a worn, well-featured face, and thinnish hair that had once been light brown, but was much faded and not a little gray in these later years. It had been thought a pity that she married John Finch, who had not half so much force as she, and with all her wisdom and affection and economy, every year had seemed to take away something from them, leaving few gifts and gains in exchange. At first her pride and ambition, which were reasonable enough, always clung to her husband's plans and purposes; but as she saw year after year that he stayed exactly in the same place, making little headway either in farming or anything else, she began to live more and more in her daughter's life, and looked eagerly to see her win her way and gain an honorable place, first in her school life, and afterward as a teacher. She had never dreamed beforehand of the difficulties that had assailed Polly since she came home the head of her class in June. She had supposed that it would be an easy thing for her now to find a good situation in a high or private school, with a capital salary. She hated to think there was nothing for her but to hold sway over the few scholars in the little unpainted school-house half a mile down the road, even though the girl, who was the very delight of her heart, should be with her so much more than they had expected at first. She was a kind, simple-hearted, good woman, this elder Mary Finch, and she had borne her failing fortunes with perfect bravery; she had been the sunshine and inspiration of the somewhat melancholy house for many years.

At last she saw her husband coming along the road, and even that far-away first glimpse of him told her that she would hear no good news. He pulled up the fallen buffalo-robe over his lap, and sat erect, and tried to look unconcerned as he drove into the yard, but it was some time before he came into the house. He unharnessed the horse with stiff and shaking hands, and gave him his supper, and turned the old wagon and backed it into its place before he came in. Polly had come home also by that time, and was sitting by the window, and did not turn to speak to him. His wife looked old, and her face was grayish, and the lines of it were hard and drawn in strange angles.

"You had better sit right down by the fire, John," she told him, "and I'll get you and Polly a good hot supper right away. I think, like's not, you didn't get a mouthful of dinner."

"I've no need to tell you I've got bad news," he said. "The bank's failed, and they won't pay more 'n ten cents on a dollar, if they make out to do that. It's worse than we ever thought it could be. The cashier got speculating, and he's made 'way with about everything."

It seemed to him as if he had known this for years, it was such an old, sad story already, and he almost wondered at the surprise and anger that his wife and Polly showed at once. It made him a little impatient that they would ask him so many eager questions. This was the worst piece of misfortune that had ever come to him. Although they had heard the day before that the bank would pass its dividend, and had been much concerned and troubled, and had listened incredulously to worse stories of the condition of the bank's finances, they had looked for nothing like this.

There was little to be said, but everything to be thought and feared. They had put entire confidence in this bank's security, and the money which had belonged to John Finch's father had always been left there to draw a good yearly interest. The farm was not very productive, and they had depended upon this dividend for a large part of their ready money. Much of their other property had dwindled away. If ever there had been a prospect of making much off the farm, something had interfered. One year a piece of woodland had been cleared at considerable expense, and on the day before its unlucky owner was to begin to haul the great stacks of fire-wood down to the little wharf in the marshes, from whence they could be carried away to market by schooners, the fire got in, and the flames of the fallen pines made a torch that lighted all that part of the country for more nights than one. There was no insurance and no remedy, and, as an old neighbor told the unhappy owner, "the woods would not grow again in his time." John Finch was a cheerful man naturally, and very sure of the success of his plans; it was rare to see him so entirely down-hearted and discouraged, but lately he had seemed to his wife somebody to be protected and looked after even more than Polly. She sometimes felt the weight of the years she had lived, and as if she must be already very old, but he was the same boyish person to her as when she had married him; it often seemed possible that he should have his life still before him. She could not believe until very lately that it was too late for him to start out on any enterprise. Time had, indeed, touched him more lightly than it had herself, though he had the face and something of the manner and faults of an elderly and unsuccessful man.

They sat together in the kitchen, which had suddenly grown dark. Mary Finch was as cold as either of her companions, and was angry with herself for her shivering and want of courage. She was almost afraid to speak at last for fear of crying; she felt strangely unstrung and weak. The two women had told John of Polly's disappointment, that the agent for the district had given the school to his own niece, a young girl from Salem, who was to board at his house, and help his wife as much as she could with the housework out of school-hours. "It's all of a piece today," groaned the farmer. "I'm sorry for ye, Polly."

"She may hear of something yet," said Mrs. Finch, making a great effort to speak cheerfully. "You know they have her name at the normal school; people are always sending there for teachers, and oftentimes one fails at the last minute through sickness, and I shouldn't wonder If Polly found a good place yet in that way."

"I declare I don't know how we shall get along," moaned Polly's father, to whom his daughter's trouble seemed only a small part of the general misfortunes. "Here's winter coming, and I'm likely to be laid up any day with my rheumatics, and I don't see how we can afford even to take a boy to work for his board and clothes. I've got a few trees I can cut, and one cow I can sell; but there are the taxes to pay, and the minister, and money to layout on fences, come spring. The farm ran behind last year, too."

Polly rose impatiently and took down a lamp from the high chimney-shelf, knocking down the match-box as she did so, which was, after all, a good deal of relief. She put the light on the floor while she picked up the scattered matches, and her mother took a good look at her, and was somehow made to feel stronger at the sight of Polly's face.

"I guess we'd all better have some supper," said the girl. "I never should feel so discouraged if I wasn't hungry. And now I'm going to tell you what I mean to do. I'm going to put right to and go to work out-doors and in, and I'm going to help father same as if I were a boy. I believe I should like farming now twice as well as teaching, and make a good deal more money at it. I haven't a gift for teaching, and I know it, but I don't mean that what I learned shall be thrown away. Now we've got hay for the stock, plenty of it, and we've got potatoes and apples and turnips and cider in the cellar, and a good pig to kill, and so there's no danger that we shall starve. I'm just as strong as I can be, and I am going right to work, at any rate until I get a school with a first-rate salary that'll be worth more than my help will here."

"I'm sure I don't want you to throw away such a good education as you've had, for us," said Mrs. Finch, sorrowfully. "I want you to be somebody, Polly, and take your right place in the world."

But Polly answered stoutly that she wasn't sure it was a good education until she saw whether it was any use to her. There were too many second-rate teachers already, and she hadn't any reason to suppose she would be a first-rate one. She believed that people had better learn to do the things they were sure to have to do. She would rather be a boy, and farm it, than teach any school she ever saw, and for this year, at any rate, she was going to see whether her book-learning wasn't going to be some help at home. "I did the best I could at school," she said, "and it was easy enough to get my lessons, but now I've come against a dead-wall. I don't see but you both need me, and I'm well and strong as anybody alive. I'd a good deal rather work at home a while than be penned up with a lot of children, and none of us more than half know what we're about. I want to think a good deal more about teaching school before I begin to try in earnest."

"I shall be glad to have you help your mother," said John Finch, disconsolately, "and we'll manage to get along somehow."

"Don't be afraid, father," responded Polly, in really cheerful tones, as if she assumed her new situation formally at that moment. She went slowly down cellar with the lamp, leaving her parents in darkness; but by this time the tea-kettle had begun to sing, and a great glow of coals showed through the front slide of the stove.

Mr. Finch lifted himself out of his chair, and stumbled about to get the lantern and light it, and then went out to feed the cattle. He still looked chilled, and as if all happiness had forsaken him. It was some little time before he returned, and the table was already set, and supper was nearly cooked and ready to be eaten. Polly had made a pot of coffee, and drank her first cup with great satisfaction, and almost without taking breath; but her father tasted his and did not seem to care for it, eating only a little food with evident effort.

"Now I thought you would relish a good cup of coffee," said his wife, with much concern; but the man answered sadly that he couldn't eat; he felt all broken down.

"It was a perishing day for you to take that long ride. It's the bleakest road round here, that marsh road is, and you hardly ate a mouthful of breakfast. I wish you had got something to warm you up before you started to come back," said his wife, looking at him anxiously. "I believe I'll get you something now," and she went to find a treasured bottle, long stored away to be used in case of chill or illness, for John Finch was a temperate man.

"I declare I forgot to milk," he said, hopelessly. "I don't know's such a thing ever happened to me before. I thought there was something else when I was out to the barn, and I sat down on the grin'-stone frame and tried to think what it was, but I couldn't."

"I'll milk," said Polly; and she whisked upstairs and replaced her best dress, which had been already turned up and well aproned, by a worn old frock which she had used on days of cleaning, or washing, or other rough work, when she had lent a hand to help her mother. It was nothing new for her, a farmer's daughter born and bred, to undertake this work, but she made a distinct change of direction that night, and as she sat milking in the cold barn by the dull light of the lantern a certain pleasure stole over her. She was not without her ambitions, but they had never flown with free wings up an imaginary career of school-teaching. "I do believe mother and I can earn money enough to take care of us," she said to herself, "and next spring I'm going to set out as much land as father will let me have with strawberries." Her thoughts never were busier than that night. The two cows looked round at her with surprise, and seemed to value her good-natured words and hurried pats as she left them. She disturbed a sleepy row of hens perched on the rail of the hay cart, and thought it was a pity there was not a better place for them, and that they should be straying about. "I'm going to read up some of the old numbers of the *Agriculturist*," she said, "and see what I can do about having eggs to sell." It more was evident that Polly was fired with a great enthusiasm, but she remembered suddenly another new great interest which was a secret as yet even from her mother. This remembrance gave her a little uneasiness.

It was still early when the supper table had been cleared away, and the milk strained and set aside in the pantry. John Finch had drawn his chair close to the stove, and when his wife and daughter sat down also, ready to begin the evening which showed so little promise of hilarity, they saw that he was crying.

"Why, father!" Polly exclaimed, half frightened, for this was something she did not remember ever seeing since she was a child. And his wife said nothing, but came and stood beside him and watched him as if the vague sense of coming trouble which had haunted her all day was going to explain itself by some terrible crisis.

"I'm all broken down," the poor man sobbed. "I used to think I was going to be somebody, and get ahead, and nothing has gone as I wanted it to. I'm in debt more than you think, and I don't know which way to look. The farm don't yield me as it used to, and I don't grudge what we've done for the girl, but it's been all we could carry, and here she's failed of getting a place to teach. Everything seems to go against us."

This was really most sad and death-like; it truly seemed as if the wheels of existence had stopped; there seemed to be nothing to follow this unhappy day but disgrace and despair. But Polly was the first to speak, and her cheeks grew very red: "Father, I don't think you have any right to speak so. If we can't make our living one way, we will another. Losing that money in the bank isn't the worst thing that could have happened to us, and now I am going to take hold with you right here at home, as I said before supper. You think there isn't much that a woman can do, but we'll see. How much do you owe?"

But John Finch shook his head sadly, and at first refused to tell. "It would have been nothing if I had had my bonds to help me out," he finally confessed, "but now I don't see how I ever can pay three hundred dollars."

In a little while he rose wearily, though it was only a little past six, and said that he must go to bed, and his wife followed him to his room as if he were a child. This breaking down was truly a most painful and frightful thing, and Polly was not surprised to be wakened from her uneasy sleep a few hours later, for she had worried and lain awake in a way that rarely happened, fearing that her father would be ill, and wondering what plans it would be best to make for his assistance in the coming year. She believed that they could do much better with the farm, and she made up her mind to be son and daughter both.

Later Mrs. Finch called her, hurriedly coming half-way up the staircase with a light. "Your father is sick," she said, anxiously. "I don't know whether it is more than a chill, but he's in great pain, and I wish we could get the doctor. Can't you wrap up warm and go over to Minton's and see if they can't send somebody?"

"There's nobody there," said Polly; "the boys are both away. I'll go myself, and get back before you begin to miss me;" and she was already dressing as fast as she could. In that quiet neighborhood she had no thought of fear; it was not like Polly to be afraid, at any rate; and after a few words to her father, and making a bright fire in the little fire-place of the bed-room, she put on her warm old hood and mittens, and her mother's great plaid shawl, and scurried away up the road. It was a mile and a half to the doctor's house, and with every step she grew more eager to reach it. The clouds had broken away somewhat, and the stars' bright rays came darting like glistening needles at one's eyes, so keen and piercing they were. The wind had gone down, and a heavy coldness had fallen upon the earth, as if the air, like water, had frozen and become denser. It seemed another world altogether, and the old dog, that had left his snug corner behind the kitchen stove to follow Polly, kept close at her side, as if he lacked his usual courage. On the ridges the cedar-trees stood up thinner and blacker than ever; the northern lights were making the sky white and strange with their mysterious light. Polly ran and walked by turns, feeling warmed and quickened by the exercise. She was not averse to the long walk at that time of night; she had a comfortable sense of the strong young life that was hers to use and command.

Suddenly she heard the sound of other footsteps besides her own on the frozen ground, and stopped, feeling for the first time anything like fear. Her first impulse was to hide, but the road was wide and unsheltered, and there was nothing to do but to go on. She thought next that it might be somebody whom she could send the rest of the way, and in another minute she heard a familiar whistle, and called out, not without relief, "Is that you, Jerry?"

The figure stopped, and answered nothing, and Polly hurried nearer, and spoke again. "For Heaven's sake, what sends you out this time o' night?" asked the young man, almost impatiently; and Polly in her turn became a little angry with him, she could not have told why.

"I'm not out for pleasure," she answered, with some spirit. "Father is taken very sick; we are afraid it is pneumonia; and I'm going for the doctor. There was nobody to send."

"I was coming up from Portsmouth today," said the young man, "and I lost the last train, so I came on a freight train with some fellows I know, and I thought I'd foot it over from the depot. We were delayed a good while or it wouldn't have been so late. There was a car off the track at Beverly."

He had turned, and, was walking beside Polly, who wondered that he had not sense enough to offer to call the doctor for her. She did not like his gallantry, and was in no mood for friendliness. She noticed that he had been drinking, but he seemed perfectly sober; it was between Jerry Minton and herself that something almost like love-making had showed itself not long before, but somehow any tenderness she had suspected herself of cherishing for him had suddenly vanished from her heart and mind.

"I was all knocked of a heap in Salem this morning to hear that the bank had failed. Our folks will lose something, but I suppose it'll about ruin your father. Seems to affect him a good deal, don't it?"

"It hasn't quite ruined us," said Polly, angrily, and walked faster and faster.

"I've been turning it over in my mind today a good deal," said Jerry. "I hope you will call on me for anything I can do, 'specially now your father's going to be laid up."

"Thank you," said Polly, stiffly; and presently she stopped in the road, and turned and looked at him in a sharp and not very admiring way.

"You might as well go home," she told him, not unkindly. "I've got to the village now, and I shall ride home with the doctor; there's no need for you to come back out of your way." And Jerry, after a feeble remonstrance, obeyed.

The doctor was used to being summoned at such hours, and when he found it was Polly Finch he dressed hurriedly, and came down, brimful of kindness and sympathy, to let her in.

He listened almost in silence to what Polly had to say of the case, and then, taking a bottle here and there from his stores in the little room that served him as his office, he fastened his great-coat, and pulled down the fur cap that had been a valiant helmet against the blows of many winter storms, and they went out together to the stable. The doctor was an elderly man and lame, and he was delighted with the brisk way in which his young companion stepped forward and helped him. The lantern that hung in the warm little stable was not very bright, but she quickly found her way about, and the horse was soon harnessed. She found that the harness needed tightening, the doctor having used it that day for another carriage, and as he saw her try it and rebuckle it, he felt a warm glow of admiration, and said to himself that not one woman in a hundred would have done such a thing. They wrapped themselves in the heavy blankets and buffalo-skins, and set forth, the doctor saying that they could not go much faster than a walk.

He was still a little sleepy, and Polly did not have much to say at first, except in answer to one or two questions which he asked about her father's condition; but at last she told him of her own accord of the troubles that had fallen upon them that day. It already seemed a week to her since the morning; she felt as if she had grown years older instead of hours.

"Your father has a bad trouble about the heart," said the doctor, hesitatingly. "I think it is just as well you should know it, and if this is pneumonia, it may go very hard with him. And if he pulls through, as I hope he will if we catch him in time, you must see to it that he is very careful all the rest of the winter, and doesn't expose himself in bad weather. He mustn't go into the woods chopping, or anything of that sort."

"I'm much obliged to you for telling me," said Polly, bravely. "I have made up my mind to stay right at home. I was in hopes to get a school, but I couldn't do it, and now I can see it was meant that I shouldn't, for mother couldn't get along without me if father's going to be sick. I keep wishing I had been a boy," — and she gave a shaky little laugh that had a very sad tone in it, — "for it seems as if father needed my help on the farm more than mother does in the house, and I don't see why he shouldn't have it," she confessed, filled with the courage of her new opinion. "I believe that it is the only thing for me to do. I always had a great knack at making things grow, and I never should be so happy anywhere as working out-doors and handling a piece of land. I'd rather work with a hoe than a ferule any day," and she gave the queer little laugh again. Nobody would have suspected she found it so hard to bear the doctor's bad news.

"But what is it you mean to do?" asked the doctor, in a most respectful tone, though he was inwardly much amused.

Polly hesitated. "I have been thinking that we might raise a good many more early vegetables, and ever so much more poultry. Some of our land is so sheltered that it is very early, you know, and it's first-rate light loam. We always get peas and potatoes and beans long before the Mintons and the rest of the people down our way, and there's no trouble about a market."

"But you'll have to hire help," the doctor suggested.

And Polly answered that she had thought of that, but she knew she could manage some how. "It's a new thing, you see, doctor," she said, much encouraged by his evident interest, "but I mean to work my way through it. Father has sold wood and sold hay, and if we had too much butter or too many eggs, and more early potatoes than we wanted, he would sell those; but it seemed as if the farm was there only to feed us, and now I believe I can make it feed a good many other people besides; and we must get money somehow. People let girls younger than I get married, and nobody thinks it is any risk to let them try housekeeping. I'm going to try farm-keeping."

The old doctor laughed. "You've got a wise head for such a young one," he said, "and now I'll help you every way I can. I'm not a rich man, but I'm comfortably off for a country doctor, and I've got more money put away than I am likely to use; so, if you fall short at any time, you just come and tell me, and nobody shall know anything about it, and you can take your own time to pay it back. I know more about doctoring than I do about farming, or I'd give you plenty of advice. But you go ahead, Polly."

Polly nestled down into the buffaloes, feeling already that she had become a businesswoman. The old wagon bumped and shook as they went along, and in the dim light Polly caught sight of the barberry bush — only a darker shadow on the high bank at the side of the road — and she thought of it affectionately as if it were a friend. Young Minton, whom they overtook at last, called out loudly some good wish that they might find Mr. Finch better, and the doctor asked sharply who he was, as they drove by. Polly told him, not without a feeling of embarrassment, which was very provoking to her.

"I must say I never liked that tribe," said the doctor, hastily. "I always hate to have them send for me."

When they reached the farm, Polly urged the doctor to go into the house at once. There was a bright light in the kitchen and in the bedroom that opened out of it, and the girl was almost afraid to go in after she had led the horse into the barn and covered him with the blanket. The old sorrel was within easy reach of the overhanging edge of the haymow, and she left him munching comfortably. As she opened the inner door of the kitchen she heard her father's voice, weak and sharp, and the doctor speaking in assuring tones with hearty strength, but the contrast of the two voices sounded very sad to Polly. It seemed to her as if she had been gone a great while, and she feared to look at her father lest he might have changed sadly. As she came to the bedroom door, the sight of her rosy-cheeked and eager, sorry face seemed to please him, and his own face brightened.

"You're a good girl, Polly," said he. "I'm sorry you had such a bad time." He looked very ill already, and Polly could not say anything in answer. She rebuilt the fire, and then went to stand by the table, as she used when she was a little child, to see the doctor take out his doses of medicine.

Very early in the morning Jerry Minton's mother came knocking at the door, which Polly had locked after the doctor had gone away in the night. She had pushed the bolt with unwonted care, as if she wished to bar the entrance to any further trouble that might be lying in wait for them outside. Mrs. Minton was ready with her expressions of sympathy, but somehow Polly wished she would go away. She took a look at the sick man, who was sleeping after the suffering and wakefulness of the night, and shook her head ominously, for which Polly could have struck her. She was an unpleasant, croaking sort of woman, and carried in her whole manner a consciousness of the altered fortunes of the Finches; and she even condoled with Polly on her disappointment about the school.

"Jerry spoke about meeting you going for the doctor," she said in conclusion. "I told him I didn't know what you would think about catching him out so late at night; but he was to Portsmouth, and mistook the time of the train. I've been joking him for some time past. I've about made up my mind there's some attraction to Portsmouth. He was terrible took with that Miss Hallett who was stopping to the minister's in the summer."

This was more than Polly could bear, for it was only a short time since Mrs. Minton had been paying her great attention, and wishing that she and Jerry would make a match of it, as the farms joined, and the farm-work was growing too heavy for her as she became older.

"If you mean Mary Hallett, she was married in September to a young man in Boston, partner in a commission firm," said Polly; and Mrs. Minton, for that time at any rate, was routed horse and foot.

"I hate that woman!" she said, angrily, as she shut the door, not very gently, after her.

It was a long, hard illness that followed, and the younger and the elder Mary Finch were both tired and worn out before it ended in a slow convalescence that in its dangers and troubles was almost as bad as the illness itself. The doctor was most kind and helpful in other ways than with his medicines. It was a most cheerful and kindly presence, and more than once Polly drove back to the village with him, or went with her own horse to bring him to the farm, and they became fast friends. The girl knew without being told that it would be a long time before her father would grow strong again, if that time ever came at all. They had got on very well without help, she and her mother. Some of the neighbors had offered their services in-doors and out, but these latter offers were only occasionally accepted.

The oxen had been hired by a man who was hauling salt hay to town, and Polly had taken care of the horse and the two cows. She had split the firewood and brought it in, and had done what little rough work had to be attended to in these weeks in spite of her mother's unwillingness. To tell the truth, she enjoyed it after the heat and stillness of the house, and when she could take the time to run out for a little while, it was always to take a look at some part of the farm, and though many of her projects proved to be castles in the air, she found almost her only pleasure in these sad winter days in building them and thinking them over.

Before her father's illness she would have turned most naturally to Jerry Minton for help and sympathy, for he had made himself very kind and pleasant to her then. Polly had been thought a good match, since she was an only child, and it was everywhere known that John Finch and his wife had both inherited money. Besides, it gave the more dignity to her position that she had been so long away at school, and such good accounts of her standing there had reached her native place; and Polly was uncommonly good-looking, if the truth must be told, which Jerry Minton's eyes had been quick to notice. Though it was known at once through the town what a plight the Finches' affairs were in, Jerry had come at first, apparently unconscious of his mother's withdrawal of his attentions, with great show of sympathy and friendliness, to offer to watch with the sick man by night, or to be of any use by day, and he had been much mortified and surprised at Polly's unmistakable repulse. Her quick instinct had detected an assumption of condescension and patronage on his part as well as his mother's, and the growing fondness which she had felt earlier in that season turned to a dislike that grew much faster in the winter days. Her mother noticed the change in her manner, and one night as they sat together in the kitchen Mrs. Finch whispered a gentle warning to her daughter. "I thought one time that there might be something between you and Jerry," she said. "I hope you won't let your duty to your father and me stand in the way of your settling yourself comfortably. I shouldn't like to think we were going to leave you alone. A woman's better to have a home of her own."

Polly turned so red that her mother could see the color even in the dim light by which they watched.

"Don't you worry about me," said the girl, "This is my home, and I wouldn't marry Jerry Minton if he were the President."

That was a black and snowless winter until late in January. There, near the sea, such seasons are not so uncommon as they are farther inland; but the desolation of the landscape struck Polly Finch all the more forcibly since it was answered to by the anxiety and trouble that had fallen into her life. She had not been at home in midwinter for several years before, and in those earlier days she had never noticed the outward world as she had learned to do as she grew older. The farm was a pleasant group of fields in summer, lying among the low hills that kept away both the winds from the sea and the still keener and bitterer northwest wind. Yet the plain, warm, story-and-a-half house, with its square front yard, with lilac and rose bushes, and the open side yard with its close green turf, and the barns and outbuildings beyond, was only a little way from the marshes. From Polly's own upper window there was an outlook that way over a low slope of one of the pasture hills, and sometimes when she felt tired and dreary, and looked out there, it seemed to her as if the half-dozen black cedars were standing there watching the house, and waiting for a still greater sorrow and evil fortune to go in at the door. Our heroine's life was not a little lonely, and it would have been much worse if she had not been so busy and so full of care. She missed the girls who had been her companions at school, and from having her duties marked out for her by her teachers, and nothing to do but to follow set tasks, and do certain things at certain hours, it was a great change to being her own mistress, charged with not only her own but other people's welfare.

The women from the few neighboring houses who came in to pay friendly visits, or to help with the housework, said very good things about Polly afterward. It had been expected that she would put on at least a few fine airs, but she was so dutiful, and worked so hard and so sensibly, and with such manifest willingness and interest, that no one could help praising her. A very old neighbor, who was still mindful of the proprieties of life, though she had become too feeble to be of much practical use in the event of a friend's illness, came one afternoon to pay a visit. She was terribly fatigued after the walk which had been so long for her, and Polly waited upon her kindly, and brought her some refreshments, all in the middle of one of her busiest afternoons. Poor old

Mrs. Wall! she made her little call upon the sick man, who was almost too weak to even show his gratitude that she had made so great an effort to keep up the friendly custom, and after saying sadly that she used to be a great hand to tend the sick, but her day was over, she returned to the kitchen, when Polly drew the big rocking-chair to the warmest corner, and entertained her to the best of her power. The old woman's eye fell upon a great pile of newspapers.

"I suppose you are a great hand to read, after all your schooling?" and Polly answered that she did like to read very much, and added: "Those are old numbers of the *Agriculturist*. Father has taken it a good many years, and I've taken to studying farming."

Mrs. Wall noticed the little blush that followed this announcement, and did not question its seriousness and truthfulness.

"I'm going to help father carry on the farm," said Polly, suddenly, fearing that her guest might think she meant to marry, and only take the in-door part of the farm's business.

"Well, two heads are better than one," said the old lady, after a minute's reflection; "only an old horse and a young one don't always pull well together. But I can see, if my eyes aren't what they used to be, that you are a good smart girl, with some snap to ye. I guess you've got power enough to turn 'most any kind of a mill. There was my own first cousin Serena Allen, her husband was killed in the last war, and she was left with two children when she wasn't a great deal older than you be, and she run the farm, and lived well, and laid up a handsome property. She was some years older than I, but she hasn't been dead a great many years. She'd plow a piece of ground as well as a man. They used to call her Farmer Allen. She was as nice a woman as I ever knew."

Polly laughed more heartily than she had for a good while, and it did her father good to hear her; but later, when the visitor had gone, in spite of Polly's offer to drive her home a little later when another neighbor returned the horse, our friend watched her go away with feeble steps, a bent, decrepit figure, almost worn out with spending so many years in a world of hard work. She might have stood for a picture of old age, and Polly felt it as she stood at the window. It had never come home to her thoroughly before, the inevitableness of growing old, and of the limitation of this present life; how soon the body loses its power, and the strength of the mind wanes with it. All that old Mrs. Wall could do in this world was done, and her account was virtually closed. "Here I am just starting out," said unlucky John Finch's only daughter. "I did think I might be going to have a great career sometimes when I was at school, and here I am settling down just like everybody else, and only one wave, after all, instead of being a whole tide. And it isn't going to be a great while before I have as hard work to get up that little hill as old Mrs. Wall. But I'm going to beat even her cousin Serena Allen. I am going to be renowned as Farmer Finch."

Polly found it very hard to wait until it should be time to make her garden and plant it, and every day made her more impatient, while she plied her father with questions, and asked his opinion so many times as to the merits of different crops, that he was tired of the subject altogether. Through many seasons he had tried these same experiments, with not very great success, and he could not imagine the keen interest and enthusiasm with which Polly's soul was fired. She had never known such a late spring, and the scurries of snow in March and early April filled her with dismay, as if each had blighted and frost-bitten her whole harvest. The day the garden was plowed was warm and spring-like, and John Finch crept out slowly, with his stick held fast in a pale and withered-looking hand, to see the work go on. He groaned when he saw what a great piece of ground was marked out by the long first furrows, and felt a new sense of his defeated and weak condition. He began to protest angrily at what he believed to be his daughter's imprudent nonsense, but the thought struck him that Polly might know what she was about better than he did, and he fell back contentedly upon his confidence in her, and leaned on the fence in the sun, feeling very grateful that somebody else had taken things in charge, he was so dull and unequal to making any effort. "Polly's got power," he told himself several times that day, with great pride and satisfaction.

As the summer went on, and early potatoes from the Finch farm were first in the market, though everybody who saw them planted had believed they would freeze and never grow, and the other crops had sometimes failed, but for the most part flourished famously, Polly began to attract a good deal of attention, for she manifested uncommon shrewdness and business talent, and her enterprise, held in check by her father's experience, wrought wonders in the garden and fields. Over and over John Finch said, admiringly, to his wife, "How Polly does take hold of things!" and while he was quick to see the objections to her plans, and had failed in his own life affairs because he was afraid to take risk, he was easily persuaded into thinking it was worth while to do the old work in new ways. It was lucky that Polly had a grand capital of strength to live upon, for she gave herself little rest all summer long; she was up early every morning and hard at work, and only wished that the days were twice as long. She minded neither heat nor rain, and having seen her way clear to employ a strong country boy whom the doctor had met in his rounds and recommended, she took care of the great garden with his help; and when she had occasion to do battle with the market-men who came foraging that way, she came off victorious in the matter of fair prices.

Now that so much has been said about the days and the thoughts that led to the carrying out of so bold a scheme, it is a pity there is not time enough to give a history of the struggles and successes of that first summer. There never was a young man just "out of his time" and rejoicing in his freedom, who went to work more diligently and eagerly than Polly Finch, and few have set their wits at work on a New England farm half so intelligently. She managed a great flock of poultry with admirable skill. Her geese walked in a stately procession all that summer to and from their pleasure-ground at the edge of the marsh, and not a hen that stole her nest but was tracked to earth like a fox and cooped triumphantly. She tinkered the rickety bee-hives that stood in a long and unremunerative row in the garden until the bees became good housekeepers and excellent providers for very shame. She gathered more than one of the swarms herself without a sting, and by infinite diligence she waged war successfully on the currant worms, with the result that she had a great crop of currants when everybody else's came to grief. She wondered why the butter that she and her mother made brought only a third-rate price, and bought a pound of the very best for a pattern, and afterward was sparing of salt, and careful to churn while the cream was sweet and fresh. She sold the oxen, and bought another horse instead for the lighter team, which would serve her purpose better, and every morning, after the crops began to yield, a wagon-load of something or other went from the farm to market.

She was as happy as a queen, and as well and strong as girls ought to be; and though some people laughed a good deal, and thought the ought to be ashamed to work on the farm like a man, they were forced to like her all the better when they saw her; and when she came into church on Sunday, nobody could have said that she had become unwomanly and rough. Her hands grew to need a larger pair of gloves than she was used to wearing, but that did not trouble her; and she liked a story-book, or a book with more lessons in it still, better than ever she had. Two girls who had been her best friends at school came in the course of the summer to visit her, and were asked out into the garden, after the early breakfast, because she must weed the beets, and after sitting still for a while on a garden bench, they began to help her, and both got headaches; but at the end of the week, having caught the spirit and something of the enjoyment of her life, they would have been glad to spend the rest of the summer with her. There is something delightful in keeping so close to growing things, and one gets a great sympathy with the life that is in nature, with the flourishing of some plants and the hindered life of others, with the fruitfulness and the ripening and the gathering-in that may be watched an tended and counted on one small piece of ground.

Everything seemed to grow that she touched, and it was as if the strength of her own nature was like a brook that made everything green where it went. She had her failures and disappointments, and she reaped little in some places where she had looked for great harvests. The hay was partly spoiled by some wet weather, but there was still enough for their own stock, and they sold the poultry for double the usual money. The old doctor was Polly's firm friend, and he grew as fond of her as if she were his own daughter, and could hardly force himself to take the money she brought back in payment of a loan she had been forced to ask of him, unknown even to her mother, once when things went hard against her enterprise late in the spring.

John Finch gained strength slowly all that summer, but his heart grew lighter day by day, and he and Polly made enthusiastic plans in the summer evenings for increased sheep-raising on their widespread pasture-land, and for a great poultry-yard, which was to bring them not a little wealth. And on Thanksgiving-day, when our farmer counted up her gains finally, she was out of debt, and more than satisfied and contented. She said over and over again that she never should be happier than she had been that summer. But more than one shortsighted towns-woman wondered that she should make nothing of herself when she had had a good education, and many spoke as if Polly would have been more admirable and respectable if she had succeeded in getting the little town school teachership. She said herself that she was thankful for everything she had learned at school that had helped her about her farming and gardening, but she was not meant for a teacher. "Unless folks take a lesson from your example," said the doctor. "I've seen a good deal of human nature in my day, and I have found that people who look at things as they are, and not as they wish them to be, are the ones who succeed. And when you see that a thing ought to be done, either do it yourself or be sure you get it done. 'Here I've no school to teach, and father has lost his money and his health. We've got the farm; but I'm only a girl. The land won't support us if we let it on the halves.' That's what you might have said, and sat down and cried. But I liked the way you undertook things. The farm was going to be worked and made to pay; you were going to do it; and you did do it. I saw you mending up a bit of fence here and there, and I saw you busy when other folks were lazy. You're a good girl, Polly Finch, and I wish there were more like you," the doctor concluded. "You take hold of life in the right way. There's plenty of luck for you in the world. And now I'm going to let you have some capital this next spring, at a fair interest, or none, and you can put yourself in a way to make something handsome."

This is only a story of a girl whom fate and fortune seemed to baffle; a glimpse of the way in which she made the best of things, and conquered circumstances, instead of being what cowards call the victim of circumstances. Whether she will live and die as Farmer Finch, nobody can say, but it is not very likely. One thing is certain: her own character had made as good a summer's growth as anything on her farm, and she was ashamed to remember that she had ever thought seriously of loving Jerry Minton. It will be a much better man than he whom she falls in love with next. And whatever may fall to her lot later, she will always be glad to think that in that sad emergency she had been able to same her father and mother from anxiety and despair, and that she had turned so eagerly and readily to the work that was useful and possible when her own plans had proved impossible, and her father's strength had failed.

All that is left to be said of this chapter of her story is that one day when she was walking to the village on one of her rare and happy holidays she discovered that, in widening a bit of the highway, her friend the little barberry bush was to be uprooted and killed. And she took a spade that was lying idle, the workmen having gone down the road a short distance, and dug carefully around the roots, and put her treasure in a safe place by the wall. When she returned, later in the day, she shouldered it, thorns and all, and carried it home, and planted it in an excellent situation by the orchard fence; and there it still grows and flourishes. I suppose she will say to herself as long as she lives, when things look ugly and troublesome, "I'll see if the other side is any better, like my barberry bush."

❦ MARSH ROSEMARY ❧

Part I.

ONE HOT AFTERNOON IN August, a single moving figure might have been seen following a straight road that crossed the salt-marshes of Walpole. Everybody else had either stayed at home or crept into such shade as could be found near at hand. The thermometer marked at least ninety degrees. There was hardly a fishing-boat to be seen on the glistening sea, only far away on the hazy horizon two or three coasting schooners looked like ghostly flying Dutchmen, becalmed for once and motionless.

Ashore, the flaring light of the sun brought out the fine, clear colors of the level landscape. The marsh grasses were a more vivid green than usual, the brown tops of those that were beginning to go to seed looked almost red, and the soil at the edges of the tide inlets seemed to be melting into a black, pitchy substance like the dark pigments on a painter's palette. Where the land was higher the hot air flickered above it dizzily. This was not an afternoon that one would naturally choose for a long walk, yet Mr. Jerry Lane stepped briskly forward, and appeared to have more than usual energy. His big boots trod down the soft carpet of pussy clover that bordered the dusty, whitish road. He struck at the stationary procession of thistles with a little stick as he went by. Flight after flight of yellow butterflies fluttered up as he passed, and then settled down again to their thistle flowers, while on the shiny cambric back of Jerry's Sunday waistcoat basked at least eight large green-headed flies in complete security.

It was difficult to decide why the Sunday waistcoat should have been put on that Saturday afternoon. Jerry had not thought it important to wear his best boots or best trousers, and had left his coat at home altogether. He smiled as he walked along, and once when he took off his hat, as a light breeze came that way, he waved it triumphantly before he put it on again. Evidently this was no common errand that led him due west, and made him forget the hot weather, and caused him to shade his eyes with his hand, as he looked eagerly at a clump of trees and the chimney of a small house a little way beyond the boundary of the marshes, where the higher ground began.

Miss Ann Floyd sat by her favorite window, sewing, twitching her thread less decidedly than usual, and casting a wistful glance now and then down the road or at the bees in her gay little garden outside. There was a grim expression overshadowing her firmly-set, angular face, and the frown that always appeared on her forehead when she sewed or read the newspaper was deeper and straighter than usual. She did not look as if she were conscious of the heat, though she had dressed herself in an old-fashioned skirt of sprigged lawn and a loose jacket of thin white dimity with out-of-date flowing sleeves. Her sandy hair was smoothly brushed; one lock betrayed a slight crinkle at its edge, but it owed nothing to any encouragement of Nancy Floyd's. A hard, honest, kindly face this was, of a woman whom everybody trusted, who might be expected to give of whatever she had to give, good measure, pressed down and running over. She was a lonely soul; she had no near relatives in the world. It seemed always as if nature had been mistaken in not planting her somewhere in a large and busy household.

The little square room, kitchen in winter and sitting-room in summer, was as clean and bare and thrifty as one would expect the dwelling-place of such a woman to be. She sat in a straight-backed, splint-bottomed kitchen chair, and always put back her spool with a click on the very same spot on the window-sill. You would think she had done with youth and with love affairs, yet you might as well expect the ancient cherry-tree in the corner of her yard to cease adventuring its white blossoms when the May sun shone! No woman in Walpole had more bravely and patiently borne the burden of loneliness and lack of love. Even now her outward behavior gave no hint of the new excitement and delight that filled her heart.

"Land sakes alive!" she says to herself presently, "there comes Jerry Lane. I expect, if he sees me settin' to the winder, he'll come in an' dawdle round till supper time!" But good Nancy Floyd smooths her hair hastily as she rises and drops her work, and steps back toward the middle of the room, watching the gate anxiously all the time. Now, Jerry, with a crestfallen look at the vacant window, makes believe that he is going by, and takes a loitering step or two onward, and then stops short; with a somewhat sheepish smile he leans over the neat picket fence and examines the blue and white and pink larkspur that covers most of the space in the little garden. He takes off his hat again to cool his forehead, and replaces: it, without a grand gesture this time, and looks again at the window hopefully.

There is a pause. The woman knows that the man is sure she is there; a little blush colors her thin cheeks as she comes boldly to the wide-open front door.

"What do you think of this kind of weather?" asks Jerry Lane, complacently, as he leans over the fence, and surrounds himself with an air of self-sacrifice.

"I call it hot," responds the Juliet from her balcony, with deliberate assurance, "but the corn needs sun, everybody says. I shouldn't have wanted to toil up from the shore under such a glare, if I had been you. Better, come in and set a while, and cool off," she added, without any apparent enthusiasm. Jerry was sure to come, any way. She would rather make the suggestion than have him.

Mr. Lane sauntered in, and seated himself opposite his hostess, beside the other small window, and watched her admiringly as she took up her sewing and worked at it with great spirit and purpose. He clasped his hands together and leaned forward a little. The shaded kitchen was very comfortable, after the glaring light outside, and the clean orderliness of the few chairs and the braided rugs and the table under the clock, with some larkspur and asparagus in a china vase for decoration, seemed to please him unexpectedly. "Now just see what ways you women folks have of fixing things up, smart!" he ventured gallantly.

Nancy's countenance did not forbid further compliment; she looked at the flowers herself, quickly, and explained that she had gathered them a while ago to send to the minister's sister, who kept house for him. "I saw him going by, and expected he'd be back this same road. Mis' Elton's be'n havin' another o' her dyin' spells this noon, and the deacon went by after him hot foot. I'd souse her well with stone-cold water. She never sent for me to set up with her; she knows better. Poor man, 't was likely he was right into the middle of tomorrow's sermon. 'T ain't considerate of the deacon, and when he knows he's got a fool for a wife, he needn't go round persuading other folks she's so suffering as she makes out. They ain't got no larkspur this year to the parsonage, and I was going to let the minister take this over to Amandy; but I see his wagon over on the other road, going towards the village, about an hour after he went by here."

It seemed to be a relief to tell somebody all these things after such a season of forced repression, and Jerry listened with gratifying interest. "How you do see through folks!" he exclaimed in a mild voice. Jerry could be very soft spoken if he thought best. "Mis' Elton's a die-away lookin' creatur'. I heard of her saying last Sunday, comin' out o' meetin', that she made an effort to git there once more, but she expected 't would be the last time. Looks as if she eat well, don't she?" he concluded, in a meditative tone.

"Eat!" exclaimed the hostess, with snapping eyes. "There ain't no woman in town, sick or well, can lay aside the food that she does. 'Tain't to the table afore folks, but she goes seeking round in the cupboards half a dozen times a day. An' I've heard her remark 't was the last time she ever expected to visit the sanctuary as much as a dozen times within five years."

"Some places I've sailed to they'd have hit her over the head with a club long ago," said Jerry, with an utter lack of sympathy that was startling. "Well, I must be gettin' back again. Talkin' of eatin' makes us think o' supper time. Must be past five, ain't it? I thought I'd just step up to see if there wa'n't anything I could lend a hand about, this hot day."

Sensible Ann Floyd folded her hands over her sewing, as it lay in her lap, and looked straight before her without seeing the pleading face of the guest. This moment was a great crisis in her life. She was conscious of it, and knew well enough that upon her next words would depend the course of future events. The man who waited to hear what she had to say was indeed many years younger than she, was shiftless and vacillating. He had drifted to Walpole from nobody knew where, and possessed many qualities which she had openly rebuked and despised in other men. True enough, he was good-looking, but that did not atone for the lacks of his character and reputation. Yet she knew herself to be the better man of the two, and since she had surmounted many obstacles already she was confident that, with a push here and a pull there to steady him, she could keep him in good trim. The winters were so long and lonely; her life was in many ways hungry and desolate in spite of its thrift and conformity. She had laughed scornfully when he stopped, one day in the spring, and offered to help her weed her garden; she had even joked with one of the neighbors about it. Jerry had been growing more and more friendly and pleasant ever since. His ease-loving careless nature was like a comfortable cushion for hers, with its angles, its melancholy anticipations and self-questionings. But Jerry liked her, and if she liked him and married him, and took him home, it was nobody's business; and in that moment of surrender to Jerry's cause she arrayed herself at his right hand against the rest of the world, ready for warfare with any and all of its opinions.

She was suddenly aware of the sunburnt face and light, curling hair of her undeclared lover, at the other end of the painted table with its folded leaf. She smiled at him vacantly across the larkspur; then she gave a little start, and was afraid that her thoughts had wandered longer than was seemly. The kitchen clock was ticking faster than usual, as if it were trying to attract attention.

"I guess I'll be getting home," repeated the visitor ruefully, and rose from his chair, but hesitated again at an unfamiliar expression upon his companion's face.

"I don't know as I've got anything extra for supper, but you stop," she said, "an' take what there is. I wouldn't go back across them marshes right in this heat."

Jerry Lane had a lively sense of humor, and a queer feeling of merriment stole over him now, as he watched the mistress of the house. She had risen, too; she looked so simple and so frankly sentimental, there was such an incongruous coyness added to her usually straightforward, angular appearance, that his instinctive laughter nearly got the better of him, and might have lost him the prize for which he had been waiting these many months. But Jerry behaved like a man: he stepped forward and kissed Ann Floyd; he held her fast with one arm as he stood beside her, and kissed her again and again. She was a dear good woman. She had a fresh young heart, in spite of the straight wrinkle in her forehead and her work-worn hands. She had waited all her days for this joy of having a lover.

Part II.

Even Mrs. Elton revived for a day or two under the tonic of such a piece of news. That was what Jerry Lane had hung round for all summer, everybody knew at last. Now he would strike work and live at his ease, the men grumbled to each other; but all the women of Walpole deplored most the weakness and foolishness of the elderly bride. Ann Floyd was comfortably off, and had something laid by for a rainy day; she would have done vastly better to deny herself such an expensive and utterly worthless luxury as the kind of husband Jerry Lane would make. He had idled away his life. He earned a little money now and then in seafaring pursuits, but was too lazy, in the shore parlance, to tend lobsterpots. What was energetic Ann Floyd going to do with him? She was always at work, always equal to emergencies, and entirely opposed to dullness and idleness and even placidity. She liked people who had some snap to them, she often avowed scornfully, and now she had chosen for a husband the laziest man in Walpole. "Dear sakes," one woman said to another, as they heard the news, "there's no fool like an old fool!"

The days went quickly by, while Miss Ann made her plain wedding clothes. If people expected her to put on airs of youth they were disappointed. Her wedding bonnet was the same sort of bonnet she had worn for a dozen years, and one disappointed critic deplored the fact that she had spruced up so little, and kept on dressing old enough to look like Jerry Lane's mother. As her acquaintances met her they looked at her with close scrutiny, expecting to see some outward trace of such a silly, uncharacteristic departure from good sense and discretion. But Miss Floyd, while she was still Miss Floyd, displayed no silliness and behaved with dignity, while on the Sunday after a quiet marriage at the parsonage she and Jerry Lane walked up the side aisle to their pew, the picture of middle-aged sobriety and respectability. Their fellow parishoners, having recovered from their first astonishment and amusement, settled down to the belief that the newly married pair understood their own business best, and that if anybody could make the best of Jerry and get any work out of him, it was his capable wife.

"And if she undertakes to drive him too hard he can slip off to sea, and they'll be rid of each other," commented one of Jerry's 'longshore companions, as if it were only reasonable that some refuge should be afforded to those who make mistakes in matrimony.

There did not seem to be any mistake at first, or for a good many months afterward. The husband liked the comfort that came from such good housekeeping, and enjoyed a deep sense of having made a good anchorage in a well-sheltered harbor, after many years of thriftless improvidence and drifting to and fro. There were some hindrances to perfect happiness: he had to forego long seasons of gossip with his particular friends, and the outdoor work which was expected of him, though by no means heavy for a person of his strength, fettered his freedom not a little. To chop wood, and take care of a cow, and bring a pail of water now and then, did not weary him so much as it made him practically understand the truth of weakly Sister Elton's remark that life was a constant chore. And when poor Jerry, for lack of other interest, fancied that his health was giving way mysteriously, and brought home a bottle of strong liquor to be used in case of sickness, and placed it conveniently in the shed, Mrs. Lane locked it up in the small chimney cupboard where she kept her camphor bottle and her opodeldoc and the other family medicines. She was not harsh with her husband. She cherished him tenderly, and worked diligently at her trade of tailoress, singing her hymns gaily in summer weather; for she never had been so happy as now, when there was somebody to please beside herself, to cook for and sew for, and to live with and love. But Jerry complained more and more in his inmost heart that his wife expected too much of him. Presently he resumed an old habit of resorting to the least respected of the two country stores of that neighborhood, and sat in the row of loafers on the outer steps. "Sakes alive," said a shrewd observer one day, "the fools set there and talk and talk about what they went through when they follered the sea, till when the women-folks comes tradin' they are obleeged to climb right over 'em."

But things grew worse and worse, until one day Jerry Lane came home a little late to dinner, and found his wife unusually grim-faced and impatient. He took his seat with an amiable smile, and showed in every way his determination not to lose his temper because somebody else had. It was one of the days when he looked almost-boyish and entirely irresponsible. His hair was handsome and curly from the dampness of the east wind, and his wife was forced to remember how, in the days of their courtship, she used to wish that she could pull one of the curling locks straight, for the pleasure of seeing it fly back. She felt old and tired, and was hurt in her very soul by the contrast between herself and her husband. "No wonder I am aging, having to lug everything on my shoulders," she thought. Jerry had forgotten to do whatever she had asked him for a day or two. He had started out that morning to go lobstering, but he had returned from the direction of the village.

"Nancy," he said pleasantly, after he had begun his dinner, a silent and solitary meal, while his wife stitched busily by the window, and refused to look at him, —"Nancy, I've been thinking a good deal about a project."

"I hope it ain't going to cost so much and bring in so little as your other notions have, then," she responded, quickly; though somehow a memory of the hot day when Jerry came and stood outside the fence, and kissed her when it was settled he should stay to supper, — a memory of that day would keep fading and brightening in her mind.

"Yes," said Jerry, humbly, "I ain't done right, Nancy. I ain't done my part for our livin'. I've let it sag right on to you, most ever since we was married. There was that spell when I was kind of weakly, and had a pain acrost me. I tell you what it is: I never was good for nothin' ashore, but now I've got my strength up I'm going to show ye what I can do. I'm promised to ship with Cap'n Low's brother, Skipper Nathan, that sails out o' Eastport in the coasting trade, lumber and so on. I shall get good wages, and you shall keep the whole on 't 'cept what I need for clothes."

"You needn't be so plaintive," said Ann, in a sharp voice. "You can go if you want to. I have always been able to take care of myself, but when it comes to maintainin' two, 'tain't so easy. When be you goin'?"

"I expected you would be sorry," mourned Jerry, his face falling at this outbreak. "Nancy, you needn't be so quick. 'Tain't as if I hadn't always set everything by ye, if I be wuthless."

Nancy's eyes flashed fire as she turned hastily away. Hardly knowing where she went, she passed through the open doorway, and crossed the clean green turf of the narrow side yard, and leaned over the garden fence. The young cabbages and cucumbers were nearly buried in weeds, and the currant bushes were fast being turned into skeletons by the ravaging worms. Jerry had forgotten to sprinkle them with hellebore, after all, though she had put the watering-pot into his very hand the evening before. She did not like to have the whole town laugh at her for hiring a man to do his work; she was busy from early morning until late night, but she could not do everything herself. She had been a fool to marry this man, she told herself at last, and a sullen discontent and rage that had been of slow but certain growth made her long to free herself from this unprofitable hindrance for a time, at any rate. Go to sea? Yes, that was the best thing that could happen. Perhaps when he had worked hard a while on schooner fare, he would come home and be good for something!

Jerry finished his dinner in the course of time, and then sought his wife. It was not like her to go away in this silent fashion. Of late her gift of speech had been proved sufficiently formidable, and yet she had never looked so resolutely angry as today.

"Nancy," he began, — "Nancy, girl! I ain't goin' off to leave you, if your heart's set against it. I'll spudge up and take right holt."

But the wife turned slowly from the fence and faced him. Her eyes looked as if she had been crying. "You needn't stay on my account," she said. "I'll go right to work an' fit ye out. I'm sick of your meechin' talk, and I don't want to hear no more of it. Ef *I* was a man" —

Jerry Lane looked crestfallen for a minute or two; but when his stern partner in life had disappeared within the house, he slunk away among the apple-trees of the little orchard, and sat down on the grass in a shady spot. It was getting to be warm weather, but he would go round and hoe the old girl's garden stuff by and by. There would be something goin' on aboard the schooner, and with delicious anticipation of future pleasure this delinquent Jerry struck his knee with his hand, as if he were clapping a crony on the shoulder. He also winked several times at the same fancied companion. Then, with a comfortable chuckle, he laid himself down, and pulled his old hat over his eyes, and went to sleep, while the weeds grew at their own sweet will, and the currant worms went looping and devouring from twig to twig.

Part III.

Summer went by, and winter began, and Mr. Jerry Lane did not reappear. He had promised to return in September, when he parted from his wife early in June, for Nancy had relented a little at the last, and sorrowed at the prospect of so long a separation. She had already learned the vacillations and uncertainties of her husband's character; but though she accepted the truth that her marriage had been in every way a piece of foolishness, she still clung affectionately to his assumed fondness for her. She could not believe that his marriage was only one of his makeshifts, and that as soon as he grew tired of the constraint he was ready to throw the benefits of respectable home life to the four winds. A little sentimental speech-making and a few kisses the morning he went away, and the gratitude he might well have shown for her generous care-taking and provision for his voyage won her soft heart back again, and made poor, elderly, simple-hearted Nancy watch him cross the marshes with tears and foreboding. If she could have called him back that day, she would have done so and been thankful. And all summer and winter, whenever the wind blew and thrashed the drooping elm boughs against the low roof over her head, she was as full of fears and anxieties as if Jerry were her only son and making his first voyage at sea. The neighbors pitied her for her disappointment. They liked Nancy; but they could not help saying, "I told you so." It would have been impossible not to respect the brave way in which she met the world's eye, and carried herself with innocent unconsciousness of having committed so laughable and unrewarding a folly. The loafers on the store steps had been unwontedly diverted one day, when Jerry, who was their chief wit and spokesman, rose slowly from his place, and said in pious tones, "Boys, I must go this minute. Grandma will keep dinner waiting." Mrs. Ann Lane did not show in her aging face how young her heart was, and after the schooner *Susan Barnes* had departed she seemed to pass swiftly from middle life and an almost youthful vigor to early age and a look of spent strength and dissatisfaction. "I suppose he did find it dull," she assured herself, with wistful yearning for his rough words of praise, when she sat down alone to her dinner, or looked up sadly from her work, and missed the amusing though unedifying conversation he was wont to offer occasionally on stormy winter nights. How much of his adventuring was true she never cared to ask. He had come and gone, and she forgave him his shortcomings, and longed for his society with a heavy heart.

One spring day there was news in the Boston paper of the loss of the schooner *Susan Barnes* with all on board, and Nancy Lane's best friends shook their sage heads, and declared that as far as regarded Jerry Lane, that idle vagabond, it was all for the best. Nobody was interested in any other member of the crew, so the misfortune of the *Susan Barnes* seemed of but slight consequence in Walpole, she having passed out of her former owners' hands the autumn before. Jerry had stuck by the ship; at least, so he had sent word then to his wife by Skipper Nathan Low. The *Susan Barnes* was to sail regularly between Shediac and Newfoundland, and Jerry sent five dollars to Nancy, and promised to pay her a visit soon. "Tell her I'm layin' up somethin' handsome," he told the skipper with a grin, "and I've got some folks in Newfoundland I'll visit with on this voyage, and then I'll come ashore for good and farm it."

Mrs. Lane took the five dollars from the skipper as proudly as if Jerry had done the same thing so many times before that she hardly noticed it. The skipper gave the messages from Jerry, and felt that he had done the proper thing. When the news came long afterward that the schooner was lost, that was the next thing that Nancy knew about her wandering mate; and after the minister had come solemnly to inform her of her bereavement, and had gone away again, and she sat down and looked her widowhood in the face, there was not a sadder nor a lonelier woman in the town of Walpole.

All the neighbors came to condole with our heroine, and, though nobody was aware of it, from that time she was really happier and better satisfied with life than she had ever been before. Now she had an ideal Jerry Lane to mourn over and think about, to cherish and admire; she was day by day slowly forgetting the trouble he had been and the bitter shame of him, and exalting his memory to something near saintliness. "He meant well," she told herself again and again. She thought nobody could tell so good a story; she felt that with her own bustling, capable ways he had no chance to do much that he might have done. She had been too quick with him, and alas, alas! how much better she would know how to treat him if she only could see him again! A sense of relief at his absence made her continually assure herself of her great loss, and, false even to herself, she mourned her sometime lover diligently, and tried to think herself a broken-hearted woman. It was thought among those who knew Nancy Lane best that she would recover her spirits in time, but Jerry's wildest anticipations of a proper respect to his memory were more than realized in the first two years after the schooner *Susan Barnes* went to the bottom of the sea. She mourned for the man he ought to have been not for the real Jerry, but she had loved him in the beginning enough to make her own love a precious possession for all time to come. It did not matter much, after all, what manner of man he was; she had found in him something on which to spend her hoarded affection.

Part IV.

Nancy Lane was a peaceable woman and a good neighbor, but she never had been able to get on with one fellow townswoman, and that was Mrs. Deacon Elton. They managed to keep each other provoked and teased from one year's end to the other, and each good soul felt herself under a moral microscope, and understood that she was judged by a not very lenient criticism and discussion. Mrs. Lane clad herself in simple black after the news came of her husband's timely death, and Mrs. Elton made one of her farewell pilgrimages to church to see the new-made widow walk up the aisle.

"She needn't tell me she lays that affliction so much to heart," the deacon's wife sniffed faintly, after her exhaustion had been met by proper treatment of camphor and a glass of currant wine, at the parsonage, where she rested a while after service. "Nancy Floyd knows she's well over with such a piece of nonsense. If I had had my health, I should have spoken with her and urged her not to take the step in the first place. She hasn't spoken six beholden words to me since that vagabond come to Walpole. I dare say she may have heard something I said at the time she married. I declare for 't, I never was so outdone as I was when the deacon came home and told me Nancy Floyd was going to be married. She let herself down too low to ever hold the place again that she used to have in folks' minds. And it's my opinion," said the sharp-eyed little woman, "she ain't got through with her pay yet."

But Mrs. Elton did not know with what unconscious prophecy her words were freighted.

The months passed by: summer and winter came and went, and even those few persons who were misled by Nancy Lane's stern visage and forbidding exterior into forgetting her kind heart were at last won over to friendliness by her renewed devotion to the sick and old people of the rural community. She was so tender to little children that they all loved her dearly. She was ready to go to any household that needed help, and in spite of her ceaseless industry with her needle she found many a chance to do good, and help her neighbors to lift and carry the burdens of their lives. She blossomed out suddenly into a lovely, painstaking eagerness to be of use; it seemed as if her affectionate heart, once made generous, must go on spending its wealth wherever it could find an excuse. Even Mrs. Elton herself was touched by her old enemy's evident wish to be friends, and said nothing more about poor Nancy's looking as savage as a hawk. The only thing to admit was the truth that her affliction had proved a blessing to her. And it was in a truly kind and compassionate spirit that, after hearing an awful piece of news, the deacon's hysterical wife forbore to spread it far and wide through the town first, and went down to the Widow Lane's one September afternoon. Nancy was stitching busily upon the deacon's new coat, and looked up with a friendly smile as her guest came in, in spite of an instinctive shrug as she had seen her coming up the yard. The dislike of the poor souls for each other was deeper than their philosophy could reach.

Mrs. Elton spent some minutes in the unnecessary endeavor to regain her breath, and to her surprise found she must make a real effort before she could tell her unwelcome news. She had been so full of it all the way from home that she had rehearsed the whole interview; now she hardly knew how to begin. Nancy looked serener than usual, but there was something wistful about her face as she glanced across the room, presently, as if to understand the reason of the long pause. The clock ticked loudly; the kitten clattered a spool against the table-leg, and had begun to snarl the thread around her busy paws, and Nancy looked down and saw her; then the instant consciousness of there being some unhappy reason for Mrs. Elton's call made her forget the creature's mischief, and anxiously lay down her work to listen.

"Skipper Nathan Low was to our house to dinner," the guest began. "He's bargaining with the deacon about some hay. He's got a new schooner, Skipper Nathan has, and is going to build up a regular business of freighting hay to Boston by sea. There's no market to speak of about here, unless you haul it way over to Downer, and you can't make but one turn a day."

" 'T would be a good thing," replied Nancy, trying to think that this was all, and perhaps the deacon wanted to hire her own field another year. He had underpaid her once, and they had not been on particularly good terms ever since. She would make her own bargains with Skipper Nathan, she thanked him and his wife!

"He's been down to the provinces these two or three years back, you know," the whining voice went on, and straightforward Ann Lane felt the old animosity rising within her. "At dinner time I wasn't able to eat much of anything, and so I was talking with Cap'n Nathan, and asking him some questions about them parts; and I spoke something about the mercy 't was his life should ha' been spared when that schooner, the *Susan Barnes*, was lost so quick after he sold out his part of her. And I put in a word, bein' 's we were neighbors, about how edifyin' your course had be'n under affliction. I noticed then he'd looked sort o' queer whilst I was talkin', but there was all the folks to the table, and you know he's a very cautious man, so he spoke of somethin' else. 'T wa'n't half an hour after dinner, I was comin' in with some plates and cups, tryin' to help what my stren'th would let me, and says he, 'Step out a little ways into the piece with me, Mis' Elton. I want to have a word with ye.' I went, too, spite o' my neuralgy, for I saw he'd got somethin' on his mind. 'Look here,' says he, 'I gathered from the way you spoke that Jerry Lane's wife expects he's dead.' Certain, says I, his name was in the list o' the *Susan Barnes*'s crew, and we read it in the paper. 'No,' says he to me, 'he ran away the day they sailed; he wasn't aboard, and he's livin' with another woman down to Shediac.' Them was his very words."

Nancy Lane sank back in her chair, and covered her horror-stricken eyes with her hands. " 'T ain't pleasant news to have to tell," Sister Elton went on mildly, yet with evident relish and full command of the occasion. "He said he seen Jerry the morning he came away. I thought you ought to know it. I'll tell you one thing, Nancy: I told the skipper to keep still about it, and now I've told you, I won't spread it no further to set folks a-talking. I'll keep it secret till you say the word. There ain't much trafficking betwixt here and there, and he's dead to you, certain, as much as if he laid up here in the burying-ground."

Nancy had bowed her head upon the table; the thin sandy hair was streaked with gray. She did not answer one word; this was the hardest blow of all.

"I'm much obliged to you for being so friendly," she said after a few minutes, looking straight before her now in a dazed sort of way, and lifting the new coat from the floor, where it had fallen. "Yes, he's dead to me, — worse than dead, a good deal," and her lip quivered. "I can't seem to bring my thoughts to bear. I've got so used to thinkin' — No, don't you say nothin' to the folks, yet. I'd do as much for you." And Mrs. Elton knew that the smitten fellow-creature before her spoke the truth, and forebore.

Two or three days came and went, and with every hour the quiet, simple-hearted woman felt more grieved and unsteady in mind and body. Such a shattering thunderbolt of news rarely falls into a human life. She could not sleep; she wandered to and fro in the little house, and cried until she could cry no longer. Then a great rage spurred and excited her. She would go to Shediac, and call Jerry Lane to account. She would accuse him face to face; and the woman whom he was deceiving, as perhaps he had deceived her, should know the baseness and cowardice of this miserable man. So, dressed in her respectable Sunday clothes, in the gray bonnet and shawl that never had known any journeys except to meeting, or to a country funeral or quiet holidaymaking, Nancy Lane trusted herself for the first time to the bewildering railway, to the temptations and dangers of the wide world outside the bounds of Walpole.

Two or three days later still, the quaint, thin figure familiar in Walpole highways flitted down the street of a provincial town.

In the most primitive region of China this woman could hardly have felt a greater sense of foreign life and strangeness. At another time her native good sense and shrewd observation would have delighted in the experiences of this first week of travel, but she was too sternly angry and aggrieved, too deeply plunged in a survey of her own calamity, to take much notice of what was going on about her. Later she condemned the unworthy folly of the whole errand, but in these days the impulse to seek the culprit and confront him was irresistible.

The innkeeper's wife, a kindly creature, had urged this puzzling guest to wait and rest and eat some supper, but Nancy refused, and without asking her way left the brightly lighted, flaring little public room, where curious eyes already offended her, and went out into the damp twilight. The voices of the street boys sounded outlandish, and she felt more and more lonely. She longed for Jerry to appear for protection's sake; she forgot why she sought him, and was eager to shelter herself behind the flimsy bulwark of his manhood. She rebuked herself presently with terrible bitterness for a womanish wonder whether he would say, "Why, Nancy, girl!" and be glad to see her. Poor woman, it was a work-laden, serious girlhood that had been hers, at any rate. The power of giving her whole self in unselfish, enthusiastic, patient devotion had not belonged to her youth only; it had sprung fresh and blossoming in her heart as every new year came and went.

One might have seen her stealing through the shadows, skirting the edge of a lumber-yard, stepping among the refuse of the harbor side, asking a question timidly now and then of some passer-by. Yes, they knew Jerry Lane, — his house was only a little way off; and one curious and compassionate Scotchman, divining by some inner sense the exciting nature of the errand, turned back, and offered fruitlessly to go with the stranger. "You know the man?" he asked. "He is his own enemy, but doing better now that he is married. He minds his work, I know that well; but he's taken a good wife." Nancy's heart beat faster with honest pride for a moment, until the shadow of the ugly truth and reality made it sink back to heaviness, and the fire of her smoldering rage was again kindled. She would speak to Jerry face to face before she slept, and a horrible contempt and scorn were ready for him, as with a glance either way along the road she entered the narrow yard, and went noiselessly toward the window of a low, poor-looking house, from whence a bright light was shining out into the night.

Yes, there was Jerry, and it seemed as if she must faint and fall at the sight of him. How young he looked still! The thought smote her like a blow. They never were mates for each other, Jerry and she. Her own life was waning; she was an old woman.

He never had been so thrifty and respectable before; the other woman ought to know the savage truth about him, for all that! But at that moment the other woman stooped beside the supper table, and lifted a baby from its cradle, and put the dear, live little thing into its father's arms. The baby was wide awake, and laughed at Jerry, who laughed back again, and it reached up to catch at a handful of the curly hair which had been poor Nancy's delight.

The other woman stood there looking at them, full of pride and love. She was young, and trig, and neat. She looked a brisk, efficient little creature. Perhaps Jerry would make something of himself now; he always had it in him. The tears were running down Nancy's cheeks; the rain, too, had begun to fall. She stood there watching the little household sit down to supper, and noticed with eager envy how well cooked the food was, and how hungrily the master of the house ate what was put before him. All thoughts of ending the new wife's sin and folly vanished away. She could not enter in and break another heart; hers was broken already, and it would not matter. And Nancy Lane, a widow indeed, crept away again, as silently as she had come, to think what was best to be done, to find alternate woe and comfort in the memory of the sight she had seen.

The little house at the edge of the Walpole marshes seemed full of blessed shelter and comfort the evening that its forsaken mistress came back to it. Her strength was spent; she felt much more desolate now that she had seen with her own eyes that Jerry Lane was alive than when he was counted among the dead. An uncharacteristic disregard of the laws of the land filled this good woman's mind. Jerry had his life to live, and she wished him no harm. She wondered often how the baby grew. She fancied sometimes the changes and conditions of the far-away household. Alas! she knew only too well the weakness of the man, and once, in a grim outburst of impatience, she exclaimed, "I'd rather she should have to cope with him than me!"

But that evening, when she came back from Shediac, and sat in the dark for a long time, lest Mrs. Elton should see the light and risk her life in the evening air to bring unwelcome sympathy, — that evening, I say, came the hardest moment of all, when the Ann Floyd, tailoress, of so many virtuous, self-respecting years, whose idol had turned to clay, who was shamed, disgraced, and wronged, sat down alone to supper in the little kitchen.

She had put one cup and saucer on the table; she looked at them through bitter tears. Somehow a consciousness of her solitary age, her uncompanioned future, rushed through her mind; this failure of her best earthly hope was enough to break a stronger woman's heart.

Who can laugh at my Marsh Rosemary, or who can cry, for that matter? The gray primness of the plant is made up of a hundred colors, if you look close enough to find them. This same Marsh Rosemary stands in her own place, and holds her dry leaves and tiny blossoms steadily toward the same sun that the pink lotus blooms for, and the white rose.

❧ THE DULHAM LADIES ❧

To be leaders of society in the town of Dulham was as satisfactory to Miss Dobin and Miss Lucinda Dobin as if Dulham were London itself. Of late years, though they would not allow themselves to suspect such treason, the most ill-bred of the younger people in the village made fun of them behind their backs, and laughed at their treasured summer mantillas, their mincing steps, and the shape of their parasols.

They were always conscious of the fact that they were the daughters of a once eminent Dulham minister; but beside this unanswerable claim to the respect of the First Parish, they were aware that their mother's social position was one of superior altitude. Madam Dobin's grandmother was a Greenaple, of Boston. In her younger days she had often visited her relatives, the Greenaples and Hightrees, and in seasons of festivity she could relate to a select and properly excited audience her delightful experiences of town life. Nothing could be finer than her account of having taken tea at Governor Clovenfoot's on Beacon Street in company with an English lord, who was indulging himself in a brief vacation from his arduous duties at the Court of St. James.

"He exclaimed that he had seldom seen in England so beautiful and intelligent a company of ladies," Madam Dobin would always say in conclusion. "He was decorated with the blue ribbon of the Knights of the Garter." Miss Dobin and Miss Lucinda thought for many years that this famous blue ribbon was tied about the noble gentleman's leg. One day they even discussed the question openly; Miss Dobin placing the decoration at his knee, and Miss Lucinda locating it much lower down, according to the length of the short gray socks with which she was familiar.

"You have no imagination, Lucinda," the elder sister replied impatiently. "Of course, those were the days of small-clothes and long silk stockings!" — whereat Miss Lucinda was rebuked, but not persuaded.

"I wish that my dear girls could have the outlook upon society which fell to my portion," Madam Dobin sighed, after she had set these ignorant minds to rights, and enriched them by communicating the final truth about the blue ribbon. "I must not chide you for the absence of opportunities, but if our cousin Harriet Greenaple were only living you would not lack enjoyment or social education."

Madam Dobin had now been dead a great many years. She seemed an elderly woman to her daughters some time before she left them; later they thought that she had really died comparatively young, since their own years had come to equal the record of hers. When they visited her tall white tombstone in the orderly Dulham burying-ground, it was a strange thought to both the daughters that they were older women than their mother had been when she died. To be sure, it was the fashion to appear older in her day, — they could remember the sober effect of really youthful married persons in cap and frisette; but, whether they owed it to the changed times or to their own qualities, they felt no older themselves than ever they had. Beside upholding the ministerial dignity of their father, they were obliged to give a lenient sanction to the ways of the world for their mother's sake; and they combined the two duties with reverence and impartiality.

Madam Dobin was, in her prime, a walking example of refinements and courtesies. If she erred in any way, it was by keeping too strict watch and rule over her small kingdom. She acted with great dignity in all matters of social administration and etiquette, but, while it must be owned that the parishioners felt a sense of freedom for a time after her death, in their later years they praised and valued her more and more, and often lamented her generously and sincerely.

Several of her distinguished relatives attended Madam Dobin's funeral, which was long considered the most dignified and elegant pageant of that sort which had ever taken place in Dulham. It seemed to mark the close of a famous epoch in Dulham history, and it was increasingly difficult forever afterward to keep the tone of society up to the old standard. Somehow, the distinguished relatives had one by one disappeared, though they all had excellent reasons for the discontinuance of their visits. A few had left this world altogether, and the family circle of the Greenaples and Hightrees was greatly reduced in circumference. Sometimes, in summer, a stray connection drifted Dulham-ward, and was displayed to the townspeople (not to say, paraded) by the gratified hostesses. It was a disappointment if the guest could not be persuaded to remain over Sunday and appear at church. When household antiquities became fashionable, the ladies remarked a surprising interest in their corner cupboard and best chairs, and some distant relatives revived their almost forgotten custom of paying a summer visit to Dulham. They were not long in finding out with what desperate affection Miss Dobin and Miss Lucinda clung to their mother's wedding china and other inheritances, and were allowed to depart without a single teacup. One graceless descendant of the Hightrees prowled from garret to cellar, and admired the household belongings diligently, but she was not asked to accept even the dislocated cherry-wood footstool that she had discovered in the far corner of the parsonage pew.

Some of the Dulham friends had long suspected that Madam Dobin made a social misstep when she chose the Reverend Edward Dobin for her husband. She was no longer young when she married, and though she had gone through the wood and picked up a crocked stick at last, it made a great difference that her stick possessed an ecclesiastical bark. The Reverend Edward was, moreover, a respectable graduate of Harvard College, and to a woman of her standards a clergyman was by no means insignificant. It was impossible not to respect his office, at any rate, and she must have treated him with proper veneration for the sake of that, if for no other reason, though his early advantages had been insufficient, and he was quite insensible to the claims of the Greenaple pedigree, and preferred an Indian pudding to pie crust that was, without exaggeration, half a quarter high. The delicacy of Madam Dobin's touch and preference in everything, from hymns to cookery, was quite lost upon this respected preacher, yet he was not without pride or complete confidence in his own decisions.

The Reverend Mr. Dobin was never very enlightening in his discourses, and was providentially stopped short by a stroke of paralysis in the middle of his clerical career. He lived on and on through many dreary years, but his children never accepted the fact that he was a tyrant, and served him humbly and patiently. He fell at last into a condition of great incapacity and chronic trembling, but was able for nearly a quarter of a century to be carried to the meeting-house from time to time to pronounce farewell discourses. On high days of the church he was always placed in the pulpit, and held up his shaking hands when the benediction was pronounced, as if the divine gift were exclusively his own, and the other minister did but say empty words. Afterward, he was usually tired and displeased and hard to cope with, but there was always a proper notice taken of these too often recurring events. For old times' and for pity's sake and from natural goodness of heart, the elder parishioners rallied manfully about the Reverend Mr. Dobin; and whoever his successor our colleague might be, the Dobins were always called the minister's folks, while the active laborer in that vineyard was only Mr. Smith or Mr. Jones, as the case might be. At last the poor old man died, to everybody's relief and astonishment; and after he was properly preached about and lamented, his daughters, Miss Dobin and Miss Lucinda, took a good look at life from a new standpoint, and decided that now they were no longer constrained by home duties they must make themselves a great deal more used to the town.

Sometimes there is such a household as this (which has been perhaps too minutely described), where the parents linger until their children are far past middle age, and always keep them in a too childish and unworthy state of subjection. The Misses Dobin's characters were much influenced by such an unnatural prolongation of the filial relationship, and they were amazingly slow to suspect that they were not so young as they used to be. There was nothing to measure themselves by but Dulham people and things. The elm-trees were growing yet, and many of the ladies of the First Parish were older than they, and called them, with pleasant familiarity, the Dobin girls. These elderly persons seemed really to be growing old, and Miss Lucinda frequently lamented the change in society; she thought it a freak of nature and too sudden blighting of earthly hopes that several charming old friends of her mother's were no longer living. They were advanced in age when Miss Lucinda was a young girl, though time and space are but relative, after all.

Their influence upon society would have made a great difference in many ways. Certainly, the new parishioners, who had often enough been instructed to pronounce their pastor's name as if it were spelled with one "b," would not have boldly returned again and again to their obnoxious habit of saying "Dobbin". Miss Lucinda might carefully speak to the neighbor and new-comers of "my sister, Miss Do-bin;" only the select company of intimates followed her lead, and at last there was something humiliating about it, even though many persons spoke of them only as "the ladies."

"The name was originally *D'Aubigne*, we think," Miss Lucinda would say coldly and patiently, as if she had already explained this foolish mistake a thousand times too often. It was like the sorrows in many a provincial château in the Reign of Terror. The ladies looked on with increasing dismay at the retrogression in society. They felt as if they were a feeble garrison, to whose lot it had fallen to repulse a noisy, irreverent mob, an increasing band of marauders who would overthrow all land-marks of the past, all etiquette and social rank. The new minister himself was a round-faced, unspiritual-looking young man, whom they would have instinctively ignored if he had not been a minister. The new people who came to Dulham were not like the older residents, and they had no desire to be taught better. Little they cared about the Greenaples or the Hightrees; and once, when Miss Dobin essayed to speak of some detail of her mother's brilliant opportunities in Boston high life, she was interrupted, and the new-comer who sat next her at the parish sewing society began to talk about something else. We cannot believe that it could have been the tea-party at Governor Clovenfoot's which the rude creature so disrespectfully ignored, but some persons are capable of showing any lack of good taste.

The ladies had an unusual and most painful sense of failure, as they went home together that evening. "I have always made it my object to improve and interest the people at such times; it would seem so possible to elevate their thoughts and direct them into higher channels," said Miss Dobin sadly. "But as for that Woolden woman, there is no use in casting pearls before swine!"

Miss Lucinda murmured an indignant assent. She had a secret suspicion that the Woolden woman had heard the story in question oftener than had pleased her. She was but an ignorant creature; though she had lived in Dulham twelve or thirteen years, she was no better than when she came. The mistake was in treating sister Harriet as if she were on a level with the rest of the company. Miss Lucinda had observed more than once, lately, that her sister sometimes repeated herself, unconsciously, a little oftener than was agreeable. Perhaps they were getting a trifle dull; toward spring it might be well to pass a few days with some of their friends, and have a change.

"If I have tried to do anything," said Miss Dobin in an icy tone, "it has been to stand firm in my lot and place, and to hold the standard of cultivated mind and elegant manners as high as possible. You would think it had been a hundred years since our mother's death, so completely has the effect of her good breeding and exquisite hospitality been lost sight of, here in Dulham. I could wish that our father had chosen to settle in a larger and more appreciative place. They would like to put us on the shelf, too. I can see that plainly."

"I am sure we have our friends," said Miss Lucinda anxiously, but with a choking voice. "We must not let them think we do not mean to keep up with the times, as we always have. I do feel as if perhaps — our hair" —

And the sad secret was out at last. Each of the sisters drew a long breath of relief at this beginning of a confession.

It was certain that they must take some steps to retrieve their lost ascendency. Public attention had that evening been called to their fast-disappearing locks, poor ladies; and Miss Lucinda felt the discomfort most, for she had been the inheritor of the Hightree hair, long and curly, and chestnut in color. There used to be a waviness about it, and sometimes pretty escaping curls, but these were gone long ago. Miss Dobin resembled her father, and her hair had not been luxuriant, so that she was less changed by its absence than one might suppose. The straightness and thinness had increased so gradually that neither sister had quite accepted the thought that other persons would particularly notice their altered appearance.

They had shrunk, with the reticence born of close family association, from speaking of the cause even to each other, when they made themselves pretty little lace and dotted muslin caps. Breakfast caps, they called them, and explained that these were universally worn in town; the young Princess of Wales originated them, or at any rate adopted them. The ladies offered no apology for keeping the breakfast caps on until bedtime, and in spite of them a forward child had just spoken, loud and shrill, an untimely question in the ears of the for once silent sewing society. "Do Miss Dobinses wear them great caps because their bare heads is cold?" the little beast had said; and everybody was startled and dismayed.

Miss Dobin had never shown better her good breeding and valor, the younger sister thought "No, little girl," replied the stately Harriet, with a chilly smile. "I believe that our headdresses are quite in the fashion for ladies of all ages. And you must remember that it is never polite to make such personal remarks." It was after this that Miss Dobin had been reminded of Madam Somebody's unusual headgear at the evening entertainment in Boston. Nobody but the Woolden woman could have interrupted her under such trying circumstances.

Miss Lucinda, however, was certain that the time had come for making some effort to replace her lost adornment. The child had told an unwelcome truth, but had paved the way for further action, and now was the time to suggest something that had slowly been taking shape in Miss Lucinda's mind. A young grand-nephew of their mother and his bride had passed a few days with them, two or three summers before, and the sisters had been quite shocked to find that the pretty young woman wore a row of frizzes, not originally her own, over her smooth forehead. At the time, Miss Dobin and Miss Lucinda had spoken severely with each other of such bad taste, but now it made a great difference that the wearer of the frizzes was not only a relative by marriage and used to good society, but also that she came from town, and might be supposed to know what was proper in the way of toilet.

"I really think, sister, that we had better see about having some — arrangements, next time we go anywhere," Miss Dobin said unexpectedly, with a slight tremble in her voice, just as they reached their own door. "There seems to be quite a fashion for them nowadays. For the parish's sake we ought to recognize" — and Miss Lucinda responded with instant satisfaction. She did not like to complain, but she had been troubled with neuralgic pains in her forehead on suddenly meeting the cold air. The sisters felt a new bond of sympathy in keeping this secret with and for each other; they took pains to say to several acquaintances that they were thinking of going to the next large town to do a few errands for Christmas.

A bright, sunny morning seemed to wish the ladies good-fortune. Old Hetty Downs, their faithful maid-servant and protector, looked after them in affectionate foreboding. "Dear sakes, what devil's wiles may be played on them blessed innocents afore they're safe home again!" she murmured, as they vanished round the corner of the street that led to the railway station.

Miss Dobin and Miss Lucinda paced discreetly side by side down the main street of Westbury. It was nothing like Boston, of course, but the noise was slightly confusing, and the passers-by sometimes roughly pushed against them. Westbury was a consequential manufacturing town, but a great convenience at times like this. The trifling Christmas gifts for their old neighbors and Sunday-school scholars were purchased and stowed away in their neat Fayal basket before the serious commission of the day was attended to. Here and there, in the shops, disreputable frizzes were displayed in unblushing effrontery, but no such vulgar shopkeeper merited the patronage of the Misses Dobin. They pretended not to observe the unattractive goods, and went their way to a low, one-storied building on a side street, where an old tradesman lived. He had been useful to the minister while he still remained upon the earth and had need of a wig, sandy in hue and increasingly sprinkled with gray, as if it kept pace with other changes of existence. But old Paley's shutters were up, and a bar of rough wood was nailed firmly across the one that had lost its fastening and would rack its feeble hinges in the wind. Old Paley had always been polite and bland; they really had looked forward to a little chat with him; they had heard a year or two before of his wife's death, and meant to offer sympathy. His business of hair-dressing had been carried on with that of parasol and umbrella mending, and the condemned umbrella which was his sign cracked and swung in the rising wind, a tattered skeleton before the closed door. The ladies sighed and turned away; they were beginning to feel tired; the day was long, and they had not met with any pleasures yet. "We might walk up the street a little farther," suggested Miss Lucinda; "that is, if you are not tired," as they stood hesitating on the corner after they had finished a short discussion of Mr. Paley's disappearance. Happily it was only a few minutes before they came to a stop together in front of a new, shining shop, where smirking waxen heads all in a row were decked with the latest fashions of wigs and frizzes. One smiling fragment of a gentleman stared so straight at Miss Lucinda with his black eyes that she felt quite coy and embarrassed, and was obliged to feign not to be conscious of his admiration. But Miss Dobin, after a brief delay, boldly opened the door and entered; it was better to be sheltered in the shop than exposed to public remark as they gazed in at the windows. Miss Lucinda felt her heart beat and her courage give out; she, coward like, left the transaction of their business to her sister, and turned to contemplate the back of the handsome model. It was a slight shock to find that he was not so attractive from this point of view. The wig he wore was well made all round, but his shoulders were roughly finished in a substance that looked like plain plaster of Paris.

"What can I have ze pleasure of showing you, young ladees?" asked a person who advanced; and Miss Lucinda faced about to discover a smiling, middle-aged Frenchman, who rubbed his hands together and looked at his customers, first one and then the other, with delightful deference. He seemed a very civil, nice person, the young ladies thought.

"My sister and I were thinking of buying some little arrangements to wear above the forehead." Miss Dobin explained, with pathetic dignity; but the Frenchman spared her any further words. He looked with eager interest at the bonnets, as if no lack had attracted his notice before. "Ah, yes. *Je comprends*; ze high foreheads are not now ze mode. Je prefer them, moi, yes, yes, but ze ladies must accept ze fashion; zay must now cover ze forehead with ze frizzes, ze bangs, you say. As you wis', as you wis'!" and the tactful little man, with many shrugs and merry gestures at such girlish fancies, pulled down one box after another.

It was a great relief to find that this was no worse, to say the least, than any other shopping, though the solemnity and secrecy of the occasion were infringed upon by the great supply of "arrangements" and the loud discussion of the color of some crimps a noisy girl was buying from a young saleswoman the other side of the shop.

Miss Dobin waved aside the wares which were being displayed for her approval "Something — more simple, if you please," — she did not like to say "older."

"But these are *très simple*," protested the Frenchman. "We have nothing younger;" and Miss Dobin and Miss Lucinda blushed, and said no more. The Frenchman had his own way; he persuaded them that nothing was so suitable as some conspicuous forelocks that matched their hair as it used to be. They would have given anything rather than leave their breakfast caps at home, if they had known that their proper winter bonnets must come off. They hardly listened to the wig merchant's glib voice as Miss Dobin stood revealed before the merciless mirror at the back of the shop.

He made everything as easy as possible, the friendly creature, and the ladies were grateful to him. Beside, now that the bonnet was on again there was a great improvement in Miss Dobin's appearance. She turned to Miss Lucinda, and saw a gleam of delight in her eager countenance. "It really is very becoming. I like the way it parts over your forehead," said the younger sister, "but if it were long enough to go behind the ears" — "*Non, non,*" entreated the Frenchman. "To make her the old woman at once would be cruelty!" And Lucinda who was wondering how well she would look in her turn, succumbed promptly to such protestations. Yes, there was no use in being old before their time. Dulham was not quite keeping pace with the rest of the world in these days, but they need not drag behind everybody else, just because they lived there.

The price of the little arrangements was much less than the sisters expected, and the uncomfortable expense of their reverend father's wigs had been, it was proved, a thing of the past. Miss Dobin treated her polite Frenchman with great courtesy; indeed, Miss Lucinda had more than once whispered to her to talk French, and as they were bowed out of the shop the gracious *Bong-sure* of the elder lady seemed to act like the string of a shower-bath, and bring down an awesome torrent of foreign words upon the two guileless heads. It was impossible to reply; the ladies bowed again, however, and Miss Lucinda caught a last smile from the handsome wax countenance in the window. He appeared to regard her with fresh approval, and she departed down the street with mincing steps.

"I feel as if anybody might look at me now, sister," said gentle Miss Lucinda. "I confess, I have really suffered sometimes, since I knew I looked so distressed."

"Yours is lighter than I thought it was in the shop," remarked Miss Dobin, doubtfully, but she quickly added that perhaps it would change a little. She was so perfectly satisfied with her own appearance that she could not bear to dim the pleasure of anyone else. The truth remained that she never would have let Lucinda choose that particular arrangement if she had seen it first in a good light. And Lucinda was thinking exactly the same of her companion.

"I am sure we shall have no more neuralgia," said Miss Dohin. "I am sorry we waited so long, dear," and they tripped down the main street of Westbury, confident that nobody would suspect them of being over thirty. Indeed, they felt quite girlish, and unconsciously looked sideways as they went along, to see their satisfying reflections in the windows. The great panes made excellent mirrors, with not too clear or lasting pictures of these comforted passers-by.

The Frenchman in the shop was making merry with his assistants. The two great frisettes had long been out of fashion; he had been lying in wait with them for two unsuspecting country ladies, who could be cajoled into such a purchase.

"Sister," Miss Lucinda was saying, "you know there is still an hour to wait before our train goes. Suppose we take a little longer walk down the other side of the way;" and they strolled slowly back again. In fact, they nearly missed the train, naughty girls! Hetty would have been so worried, they assured each other, but they reached the station just in time.

"Lutie," said Miss Dobin, "put up your hand and part it from your forehead; it seems to be getting out of place a little;" and Miss Lucinda, who had just got breath enough to speak, returned the information that Miss Dobin's was almost covering her eyebrows. They might have to trim them a little shorter; of course it could be done. The darkness was falling; they had taken an early dinner before they started, and now they were tired and hungry after the exertion of the afternoon, but the spirit of youth flamed afresh in their hearts, and they were very happy. If one's heart remains young, it is a sore trial to have the outward appearance entirely at variance. It was the ladies' nature to be girlish, and they found it impossible not to be grateful to the flimsy, ineffectual disguise which seemed to set them right with the world. The old conductor, who had known them for many years, looked hard at them as he took their tickets, and, being a man of humor and compassion, affected not to notice anything remarkable in their appearance. "You ladies never mean to grow old, like the rest of us," he said gallantly, and the sisters fairly quaked with joy.

"Bless us!" the obnoxious Mrs. Woolden was saying, at the other end of the car. "There's the old maid Dobbinses, and they've bought 'em some bangs. I expect they wanted to get thatched in a little before real cold weather; but don't they look just like a pair o' poodle dogs."

The little ladies descended wearily from the train. Somehow they did not enjoy a day's shopping as much as they used. They were certainly much obliged to Hetty for sending her niece's boy to meet them, with a lantern; also for having a good warm supper ready when they came in. Hetty took a quick look at her mistresses, and returned to the kitchen. "I knew somebody would be foolin' of 'em," she assured herself angrily, but she had to laugh. Their dear, kind faces were wrinkled and pale, and the great frizzes had lost their pretty curliness, and were hanging down, almost straight and very ugly, into the ladies' eyes. They could not tuck them up under their caps, as they were sure might be done.

Then came a succession of rainy days, and nobody visited the rejuvenated household. The frisettes looked very bright chestnut by the light of day, and it must be confessed that Miss Dobin took the scissors and shortened Miss Lucinda's half an inch, and Miss Lucinda returned the compliment quite secretly, because each thought her sister's forehead lower than her own. Their dear gray eyebrows were honestly displayed, as if it were the fashion not to have them match with wigs. Hetty at last spoke out, and begged her mistresses, as they sat at breakfast, to let her take the frizzes back and change them. Her sister's daughter worked in that very shop, and, though in the work-room, would be able to oblige them, Hetty was sure.

But the ladies looked at each other in pleased assurance, and then turned together to look at Hetty, who stood already a little apprehensive near the table, where she had just put down a plateful of smoking drop-cakes. The good creature really began to look old.

"They are worn very much in town," said Miss Dobin. "We think it was quite fortunate that the fashion came in just as our hair was growing a trifle thin. I dare say we may choose those that are a shade duller in color when these are a little past. Oh, we shall not want tea this evening, you remember, Hetty. I am glad there is likely to be such a good night for the sewing circle." And Miss Dobin and Miss Lucinda nodded and smiled.

"Oh, my sakes alive!" the troubled handmaiden groaned. "Going to the circle, be they, to be snickered at! Well, the Dobbin girls they was born, and the Dobbin girls they will remain till they die; but if they ain't innocent Christian babes to those that knows 'em well, mark me down for an idjit myself! They believe them front-pieces has set the clock back forty year or more, but if they're pleased to think so, let 'em!"

Away paced the Dulham ladies, late in the afternoon, to grace the parish occasion, and face the amused scrutiny of their neighbors. "I think we owe it to society to observe the fashions of the day," said Miss Lucinda. "A lady cannot afford to be unattractive. I feel now as if we were prepared for anything!"

🙑 A BUSINESS MAN 🙒

Part I.

IF A MAN CHOOSES a profession it is, or ought to be, with other desires than that of growing rich. He may wish to be skillful and learned as a means of self-development and helping his fellow-men, and if he is successful nobody has a right to sneer at him because he does not make a fortune. But when most men enter a mercantile life it is with the acknowledged purpose of making money. The world has a right, too, to look on with interest to find what they do with their money afterward. Dollars are of primary consideration to the standing of a business man, and are only secondary to a clergyman or a doctor — that is, when one judges by public rather than private conditions and indications of success. Yet the money-getter may win great wealth, and fail completely of reaching his highest value, and reward, and satisfaction as a human being.

People often said that there was something in the blood of the Cravens (their true name shall be a secret) which hungered for possession and was always seeking to gratify its love of acquisition. John Craven, the proud inheritor of a name already well known in business circles, certainly loved the thought of his thousands and hundred thousands. He felt a vast pleasure in letting his eyes glance down the columns of figures in his private account-book — a gratified sense of security and abundance which none of the fruits of his wealth had power to bestow. The fine house in which he lived, his handsome young children, all failed to be so completely rewarding to his eye and heart as the special page or two where the chief items of his property were represented by straight-stemmed fours and ones and delicately-curved threes and sixes and nines: He was a man who never directly wronged anyone, but who was determined to succeed and to make money. He thought little of his personal relation to society, and still less of his relation to the next world. All his mind was bent upon making a splendid financial success, and though early in life this end was gained, he still went on planning great gains and glories, and looked upon himself as one of the younger business men of his city, until long after he was a grandfather.

Then the tide of satisfaction seemed at last to turn. One thing after another forced him to waver and to hesitate in these great manipulations of his capital. Mr. Craven was keen and quick to grasp his business opportunities, but little things annoyed him, and he became sensitive where once he had been indifferent. He was just transferring his chief office and warehouse to a noble new building, when for the first time in his life he became seriously ill, and from necessity his eldest son was promoted temporarily to the head of the business.

It was a strange surprise when the family physician told him that he could no longer bear what he could once; that a man of his years must favor himself; and finally advised that a few months in Europe would do him the much needed good. John Craven was startled and angry at first; he had always looked forward to such a holiday, and had already enjoyed foreign sights by proxy, since his family had crossed the ocean repeatedly, like other families of their social station. But this seemed to mean only that the girls wished to go again, and at first he emphatically refused to be made the victim of such a conspiracy.

When he visited his place of business, however, after his illness, he was made somewhat low spirited. The new warehouse was occupied now, and it was fatiguingly large and noisy. Young John was getting on very well; he might be all the more use by and by if he had the chance of trying his hand now. He could not do much mischief, the elder man thought, as he sank into his great cushioned chair with a little sigh. He had meant to give orders that his familiar desk and wooden armchair should be brought from the old counting-room, but it was too late now, and to be sure they would be quite out of place in all this magnificence of plate glass and mahogany. Yes, Jack was right; this new office was in keeping with the position of the firm, and the senior partner looked into his new safe with pride and approval, and complimented his son upon the way he had managed things. The old grandfather who had trained him used to sit on a high stool, and wear a green baize jacket, in the first dingy counting-room. "He started us — he started us," said John Craven to himself; then he felt a little shaky and sat down again, saying that he would not go through the house until next day, perhaps. He had hardly got back his strength, but Jack might bring the statements. There were a number of new clerks even in the inner office, and one had a crafty, small face. "I don't like that fellow's looks," he muttered. "Who got him here, I should like to know!" But Jack responded, with wounded pride, that this was the smartest book-keeper in New York; he had been trying to get him into their employ for a year.

Somehow, for the first time John Craven was conscious that he was getting to be old. He grumbled something about the boys pulling and hauling him and his affairs, and wishing him out of their way. The pomp of the new counting-room, the self-sufficiency of Jack, dazzled and angered him not a little. He had thought it indispensable to the welfare of this great business that he should not miss a day at his desk, all through the busiest times of the year. But here was the establishment running along on its manifold and ponderous track, just as well as if he had been at the post of guidance. Well, not every man had given his affairs such a good momentum; he had only followed out the founder's principles, too, and he thought again of the sturdy grandfather in the baize jacket. After all, it was good for the son and successor; he would stand well in the row of John Cravens. Jack was married and settled. He had as handsome a house as his father's, a block higher up the avenue. The rascal had even grown a little patronizing of late, but John Craven, the elder, had no intention of being called an old man yet.

There were some questions to ask about the real estate investments that day, but Jack could not answer for these. Walter had been looking after that part of the property, and Walter was out of town. "So they had divided the responsibility between them, had they?" the father grumbled; but Jack brought a great handful of checks and papers to be signed, and the two men lunched and joked together. The firm was already larger than the senior partner approved. It was no use to talk about adding another member. But Jack took advantage of his father's smiles to suggest the admission of a brother-in-law, the husband of the youngest daughter. "I'll think it over," replied the chief, turning to look for his penholder. "No, his capital is no inducement. We're carrying sail enough for the present, unless times change for the better."

Jack went back to his own desk a little annoyed. He did not like to give up his authority. Was it only a month since the old gentleman had been away? It seemed like a year.

Part II.

John Craven took the doctor's advice, after all, and went to Europe. He had felt strangely weak and unequal to much effort ever since his illness, and he grasped at the promised renewal of his health. There was great satisfaction at meeting some of his old correspondents on the other side; he wholly enjoyed his journeyings, and was satisfied with the careful reports from home. He was proud, too, of some new outlooks and connections which he succeeded in forming. "In a business way," he was fond of saying to his wife, "the time had been well spent." But Mrs. Craven lost no chance of urging her husband to give up the business to the boys. He had overworked himself, she pleaded over and over again, it was no use to breakdown his health altogether. He knew very well now that he could not bear what he could once. The truth was, the ways of doing business were changing — these submarine telegraphs were doing as much harm as good. The time had gone by when a man could get private advices of a rise in values, and quickly increase his stock to control the market. Now, what one knew the rest knew, and it was simply a question of who could sell cheapest. John Craven talked it over again and again with idling merchants like himself.

Not long after their return the great sorrow of his life came to him in his wife's death. It was harder to bear the loss then than it ever could have been before, They had loved each other with a sober, undemonstrative affection, which was as permanent and unquestioned as the air they breathed. In the earlier years, while he was immersed, as he often said, in business cares, and the good woman was careful and troubled about many things, — her growing children, her household, and her social relations, — they had gone their separate ways without much reference to each other, satisfied with a mutual confidence and inspiration. For the first time in these later months they had sometimes spent all the hours of the days together, and had been more lover-like and affectionate than ever before. They sometimes talked in the long twilights of the English lakes or the soft sunshine of Italy about what they would do together when they reached home; and John Craven felt less annoyance at the thought of his boys' business capacity. He would have more time at home than ever before; he even grew interested in his wife's small charitable enterprises, and lent a willing ear to her confidences, and knew at last what good his generous checks had done in public and private needs. He had never found time to think much of these things. But alas, good Mrs. Craven died after a short illness, within a week or two of their arrival home, and the great house with its unpacked treasures, which they had chosen together, was left desolate.

It was harder than ever for this business man to assure himself that a man need not be old at his age; but somehow he had let go his active oversight of affairs, while he could summon no interest to fill the place of that to which he had given all his time and thought. He cared nothing for books or for art, or, saddest of all, his fashionable daughter thought, for society. He had given away much money because others expected it, but he had never given himself with his dollars. He was sometimes angry with the boys, and sometimes thankful to give up his responsibility, but he wished such relinquishment to be voluntary; it should not be taken for granted. His daughters were eager to have their share of his favor; they came to him with stories of the boys' assumption of authority and precedence. They were all dependent upon him in one way or another, and John Craven told himself more than once that he should like to see one of the crowd who had made his own way in the world. They were all respectful and affectionate. The girls told him again and again that they were so glad that their husbands were able to relieve him of care, and were men he could trust. Yes, he surely had a great deal to be thankful for; it seemed to be nobody's fault that he was laid on the shelf. Jack was sometimes overbearing and self-confident about the business. It was amazing that he himself, who had been counted one of the most daring, far-sighted, and enterprising men of his day, should be constantly made to feel that he was an old fogy and fast drifting astern of the times. Who should understand the times if not a man of his experience? As the long months went by, the days when he did not go to his office were of more and more frequent occurrence. The chief value of his presence seemed to be for the subscription lists, which by no means passed him by, and one day there was a vehement outbreak of anger against young Jack, who had ventured to suggest the propriety of a smaller sum than his father had seen fit to bestow. "You may be making money, but whose money are you making it with," the old man demanded, while Jack spoke soothingly and glanced round at the other desks. He did not look as if he would like to knock his father down, as he used in case of differences when they both were younger, and the senior partner was injured by this slighting of their present equality. "You treat me as if I were an old woman," he said, and went away. Jack was such an insufferable prig, and there was Jack's boy, who ought to be at a desk, already parading about the park with his dog cart and saddle-horses — a good for-nothing dandy. Times had changed indeed!

Part III.

When Mr. Craven did not go down town in the morning he sometimes took his stick and walked eastward along the street that made a right angle with the avenue nearest his house. He did not like to meet his acquaintances, even ladies, in business hours, but he found it amusing to watch the progress of some buildings not a great distance away. The contrast between this district and the region of his own home was very striking, though he found himself by no means in the most squalid portion of his native city. On the contrary, there was even a sort of thriftiness. John Craven had more than once complimented the good landlord, whoever he might be, of one long row of small brick houses. The occupants were evidently people of small means, but most respectable and orderly, and at the end of the block was a shop or two — a druggist's, and a gay little place which held out inducements to womankind, of thread and needles, neckties, and even letter-paper and calico prints. "Good thing, good thing," the rich ex-merchant would say approvingly, "if only the women don't waste their time, and travel way down to Stewart's for every spool of cotton."

It happened that John Craven walked slowly by one morning just as the owner of this place of business was opening his shutters. He was a bright-faced young man of two or three and twenty, and the elderly gentleman hesitated, then stopped and said good-morning.

The young man looked around cheerfully. "Good-day, sir," he answered; "can I do anything for you in my line?" And Mr. Craven smiled benignantly, without committing himself to any definite reply. "You are on time, I see," he said presently, tapping the pavement with his cane as the proprietor fastened the shutter back with a sufficient snap. There was only one window to the little store, but its contents were most alluringly arranged. "Yes, sir, time's money," answered the admiring owner of the trifling wares. "I should be glad to have you step inside," and with a glance along the street toward the avenue, Mr. Craven accepted the invitation. It was still early in the morning, he had not been sleeping well of late, and his luxurious household was hardly astir. His eldest daughter had come home with her family to keep the house for him after her mother's death. Her husband was the least prosperous of the sons or sons-in-law, and to tell the truth John Craven was not at all fond of him, and never had been.

There was something delightfully cordial and sincere in the younger merchant's hospitality. At any rate it was stronger than his guest's reasons for not accepting it, and Mr. Craven bowed gravely and went in at the door. He took no notice of anything in particular. The cheap goods did not invite his attention in detail, but he seated himself on one of the two light stools which were provided for the comfort of possible customers, and asked, looking about him in an interested way, how long the business had been established.

"Only a month or two," answered the young man, and a boyish color spread quickly over his face. "I hope there's a good chance here! I don't see why I shouldn't do well. I seem to have the good-will of the neighborhood, so far. There are some dressmakers near by who do a pile of work: one of them does stitching and finishing for Madame Blanc, and has all she can carry. I fill any orders, you know, for goods I don't carry in stock. I hope I shall do well here, and I don't mind saying I shall sell out the business when it gets to be worth anything, and strike for something better. I wish I was a little nearer the avenue. I know a fellow who keeps a first-rate class of goods up in Thirtieth Street that's getting rich. You see the seamstresses in some of the big houses give him all their trade, and about keep him going."

Mr. Craven returned the hopeful smile of his entertainer, and slowly unfastened his overcoat. He felt a little tired and lonely that morning, and did not wear the look of a prosperous man. The coat itself was a comfortable old one he had insisted upon keeping when his daughter had suggested the presentation of it to a deserving German mother to make over for her children. Somehow Mr. Craven liked to wear it in these morning walks away from the avenue. The buttons were loose, and one of them actually came off at this moment and rolled behind some boxes that were piled at the end of the counter. William Chellis the shopkeeper looked after it, but some instinct that he could hardly explain led him to ignore the trivial accident. The old gentleman looked as if he had seen better days. The button-holes of the coat were frayed, and a bit of the lining was hanging. Chellis had often seen the old fellow go by about this time in the morning, stopping once in a while to speak to some children, or to exchange greetings with the bricklayers who were tending the great mortar-box in front of the new block.

They talked together for a few minutes in a friendly way. Chellis was arranging his wares, and when the visitor rose to go he darted forward to open the door for him. "I should be pleased to have you drop in any time, sir," he said, with pleasant deference. "I hope you'll remember to mention the store if you have any ladies at home. My goods are mostly in their line."

"Do you keep pins?" asked Mr. Craven, turning back with evident pleasure, to make an investment in four papers. He could find somebody to give them to, and there was a satisfaction in putting the little package in his pocket. He was used to writing checks for his purchases, and was a little uncertain, as he took some change from his waistcoat pocket, about the state of his present finances.

"There never is much doing this time in the morning," explained the proprietor. "My customers either come toward night, or run over here at noon time. I ought to have somebody to help me, for I shut up now when I go down town to fill my orders. I want to get on as cheap as I can, though, for the present. All great things must have a beginning," he added as he opened the door the second time. There was something delightfully fresh and energetic about the young man. John Craven sighed to remember that there was a time when his own future lay all before him. The winter wind had risen and was whirling the dust and bits of paper along the bare pavement, and as he went away toward the avenue, he had to stop more than once and turn his back to the unwholesome gale. He happened to be just opposite a window at one time, where a sweet-faced young girl sat sewing busily. There were some half-finished garments on the table beside her; a very pretty girl she was, and she looked frankly up at the elderly man, and even gave him a bright smile of unconscious sympathy and friendliness.

The whole day afterward, while the wind blew and the weather was cold, and a few flakes of snow clicked against the windows, John Craven sat by the library fire trying to read newspapers and dozing and meditating by turns. He tried once or twice to allure his younger grandchildren down to keep him company, but they were needed upstairs to practice for a famous fancy ball in aid of some children's hospital. They were to have fine costumes and be prominent in the dances, and could only chatter to him of these things if they stayed. Their mother had rebuked him for staying out of doors so long on a chilly morning. He was late to breakfast, and she reproached him for making her uneasy. He might have a fall any day, or be knocked over by the passing carts.

"I should like to have my liberty," the old man answered, with more severity than was usual with him. He did not feel so old as other people seemed to consider him — life was not very amusing of late. But certainly he was much interested in his new acquaintance of the side street. "I'll watch that lad," Mr. Craven assured himself, "and by and by, if he does well, I'll let him have some capital." While, with rare sentiment, he also wondered if the nice girl who sewed by the window and the brisk young merchant were aware of each other's existence.

The question was answered no later than the next morning but one. Between the two interviews a serious trial came to our hero. He had been vastly punctual at the fortnightly meetings of a certain notable company, of which he had been chief originator, and had clung more and more of late to this one of the last of his active business duties. He felt unusually clear and capable as he entered the directors' room, but being early he was adroitly tendered a suggestion that he should resign his place on the board in favor of his son Jack. He could find no fault with the delicate manner in which this suggestion was made. There was a troublesome, decrepit old fellow, who had been in the way for half a dozen years, and it was proposed that the two senior directors should be put on a sort of retired list. The friend who spoke alluded to the annoyance Mr. Craven must receive from his feeling of obligation to attend the meetings now that he had shaken off so entirely the cares of business. He held so large an interest in the property that it would not have done to remove him from a part in its active control, except through his own agency, and John Craven, who was a proud man, told himself with a flash of anger that this was some of Jack's doings, and quietly acquiesced. "They knock the old folks on the head in the South Sea Islands," he grumbled next day, when he saw a too prompt series of resolutions on his retirement included in the financial report of his company. He wondered if his wife knew how lonely he was, and counted up with surprise the months since she had been taken away from him.

The morning afterward was clear and spring-like, and he went out earlier than usual. The pleasant weather was in itself a comfort, and he found himself taking quicker steps than usual toward the little store. It was already open, and there was a customer who turned a not unfamiliar face toward the door as Mr. Craven opened it. The two young people were talking eagerly, and both blushed a little in a pretty, conscious way, and said good-morning, as if the new-comer were an old friend. "This is a pleasanter day than when I had to come to a halt next your window," said the old gentleman, gallantly. He had been hurrying, and was glad to accept the seat which the younger man pushed toward him.

"There were a few little things I thought they could make use of at the house," said Mr. Craven presently, to explain his appearance — but he did not look about for the necessary goods. "How are you getting on?" he asked, in a benevolent and paternal fashion, and they turned to acquaint this friendly stranger with an assurance of their excellent prospects. Evidently the young people had a very particular interest in each other, and Mr. Craven became sure that their marriage depended upon young Chellis's future income. There was a debt of a few hundred dollars on the stock; it had been a tremendous venture for the fellow, and the wise old businessman shook his head, as he was made to understand the position of affairs. "If you could only pay off those accounts now," he said soberly, "so that you could be handling for yourself the money that is coming in." And young Chellis looked wistful and determined as he nodded his head in assent.

There was a painful silence of a moment or two which Chellis himself broke. "You lost a button off your coat when you were in day before yesterday morning, sir. I found it afterward and laid it by. Miss Brooks has got a needle with her now, I dare say, and she'll sew it on for you if you will let her;" and John Craven looked from one face to the other with pleased surprise. He would have been amused if he had known that they had talked about him several times, and had made up their minds that he was a bachelor who boarded somewhere in that region — a man who had seen better days, and was now poor and friendless. Miss Brooks had ventured to wish that he might have a little money which he would like to put into such a thriving and rising business venture as her lover's. But the lover had replied with deeper wisdom that the elderly stranger did not wear the look of a prosperous man. Poor John

Craven, with his houses and lands, his blocks of buildings, and his interest in a line of steamers, his manufactories, and his mortgages, and bank stocks, and railroad stocks, and his luxurious children, whom he had housed in palaces! He felt poorer, after all, than these young creatures, who still had their fortunes to make, and whose best capital was their love for each other.

But in the last few dragging years nothing had given him such a hearty pleasure as his new interest in this little enterprise of the fancy goods store on East Number Street. His cautious business instinct made him very careful to know his ground. Then one day, to young Chellis's great delight, when he was beginning to fear his creditors and look older and more troubled than usual, the kindly guest counted out a sum of money as if it were all he had in the world, and begged to go into partnership, waiving all formalities. The two men sat down together as if they were alike twenty-two, and embarked upon courageous plans for future gains. Sometimes of late, Mr. Craven — who let himself be called Mr. Brown, though his honest heart revolted from the deception — postponed his visit until after the late breakfast and spent as much of the day as he chose with his new friend. 'What sagacity of advice the old merchant imparted to the new one time would fail for describing. Chellis had long ago made up his mind that his benefactor must have had an unusual business career and been wrecked in some great financial crisis.

The situation was not without its dangers. Even the walk along East Number Street was beset with fears, and John Craven varied his line of approach from day to day. Once he beheld with dismay the entrance of one of his own housemaids upon his new place of business, as he stood behind the high desk casting up a column of figures. Luckily there was an inner room, to which he stealthily retreated with beating heart, and listened there to the loud, unmannerly tones of the woman who was at home a most soft-spoken and servile creature. But this accident did not happen again, and he felt more and more secure in the companionship of his young partner. It was surprising how his youthful zest and ambition seemed, for a time, to return; how pleased he was when an uncommonly good day's trade was reported. He shook his head when the young folks asked him to come to their wedding, but he slipped as large a bill as he dared into the bride's work-roughened little hand and stole away toward his own house. It had made him desolate to see the rooms the lovers were to live in. They had asked their benefactor to visit their new home in such a way that he could not refuse, and they told him they never could have got on so well without his help. Little Miss Brooks was not going to give up her sewing at present. She would take care of their tiny housekeeping and earn all she could in the spare time, just as she had always done. They did not seem like city people at all; they had the simple ways of country folks. And John Craven thought of them with deep affection as he sat at the head of his glittering dinner-table that night, and lifted a glass of his best wine in a shaking hand to drink secretly Mr. and Mrs. William Chellis's health and prosperity.

At last there came a time, late one spring, when the old business man seemed much feebler than he had ever before. He hardly ever went down to the great office now, and was even glad when the rare expedition was safely over with. Once or twice he took his seat at some assembly, but he was an inefficient figurehead, and was more annoyed than otherwise with the empty show of deference from his inferiors in office. Every day when it was possible, however, he paid an early visit to his young friends in East Number Street, and on many a morning when there were few customers coming in, he gave the ambitious proprietor warnings and suggestions. There was a young boy added to the force of this mercantile experiment, a lad from Vermont, whose bright face seemed to please the old gentleman, and on one of the last visits Chellis sent him home with Mr. Craven. It caused a good deal of curiosity and interest when the adventure was recounted, for he had helped the infirm guest up the high steps of one of the best avenue houses. But the morning calls were nearly done. Mr. Craven only appeared once more, and then when the owner of the little shop had gone down town. He and his young wife talked a great deal that night about their benefactor. "He's been the making of me," said Chellis to himself, sadly, as the days went by after that and his friend did not come again.

For a long time Mr. Craven's daughter had said proudly that her father was able to take an hour or two's walk early every morning;

in these late spring days she had complained fretfully that he used up all his strength in doing so much, and that he was fit for nothing all the rest of the day. At length John Craven was taken away to his country place, and before the summer was over he died. The poor rich man had almost ceased to care anything for even the dolls' shopkeeping, as he had often fondly called it, though he was still grateful for the pleasure that came to him as he dreamed of and planned for the future fortune of the happy young people in East Number Street.

His will was made some months before, and was as just to his own family and to public needs as all his dealings had been. There was one codicil which surprised his family entirely, — he left five thousand dollars to one William Chellis, in East Number Street, and among the latest of his private papers was a note to this legatee written in a trembling hand, which contrasted strangely with his former clear signatures.

> I have left something for you as a remembrance, I have no doubt that you will make your way in the world by its help and your own exertions, and I owe you something for your kindness and respect to an old man. Remember that getting money may make you poor as it has me, and can leave you at last a beggar for a little friendliness, and sympathy, and occupation. There are other things which a man needs beside wealth to make him happy. I am your grateful friend,
>
> JOHN CRAVEN.

The young man's eyes were strangely dimmed as he read. "Good heavens!" he said, awed and astonished. "I used to think sometimes that he wasn't the broken-down old fellow we took him for at first; but there he was all the time, one of the richest men in the city! How pleased he used to be some days to help behind the counter when two or three customers came in together. So that was old John Craven!"

"Perhaps our place made him think of old times, when he was just beginning, himself," hopefully answered the little wife. "I remember the first time I saw him, one windy morning when the dust blew in his face and he turned round and looked right in at the window. He made me feel real bad, he looked so lonesome and wishful. I never thought he was going to give us such a lot of money."

"He's given me something better than that, too," said young Chellis, solemnly; and when the woman beside him looked up to ask what he meant, he only kissed her and went away. There were truly many gains to be had in the world beside money, even if one's heart was set upon being, first of all, A Business Man.

❦ MARY AND MARTHA ❦

THE TWO SISTERS — the old Miss Deans, as people had begun to call them — had always lived together, and what had happened to one happened to the other. They often said that what one knew the other knew; and since they had spent their years very quietly, the things that each sister thought best worth saying had been said many times over. For all this, they were as different as they could be. Mary was Mary-like — a little too easy and loving-hearted; and Martha was Martha-like — a little too impatient with foolish folks, and forgetting to be affectionate while she tried to be what she called just. Sometimes she thought her younger sister visionary and sentimental; for Martha was, before all things, practical and straightforward, and there lurked a little pride in her heart because she did not see how Mary could get on without her own forethought and provision for their needs.

The two sisters were very much respected in the village where they lived. They sewed for their living; they were tailoresses by trade, and though they did not make so many suits of clothes since their neighbors found the ready-made clothing shops so cheap and convenient, they made little boys' first suits and stray jackets and trousers whenever they could. They mended them, too, for one or two busy neighbors who could afford to pay them. You might hear it said twenty times a year, "How should we ever get along without Mary and Martha Dean!" And more than once it had been questioned who could take their places if anything happened to the good women. Martha was usually strong and vigorous, short and thick-set in appearance, and a little given to bustling if anything particular were going on. She was an excellent hand to make over a carpet; she was an extremely judicious and sensible person. It was Martha who had been called upon to go and keep house for her townspeople when they went away. But more than one neighbor had dearly liked to have Mary Dean in the sick-room, she was so gentle and quiet, and did not insist upon doing something when there was nothing to do, as her good, anxious, willing sister did once in a while. Yet everybody called Martha a splendid nurse; she was so capable, they said; and most people liked to hear her talk to the sick, and tell them they were nervous and notional, and there wasn't anything great the matter with them, and she had seen folks twice as bad off. There was no gainsaying the fact that this treatment occasionally did good; for one thing, many friends had as much confidence in Martha Dean as in the doctor, and it was good for them that she rallied their hopes; "where there's a will there's a way" being as often true about getting well as it is about getting rich. But when tall, thin Mary, with her pleased, absentminded look, stole into a bedroom on a dreary day and said nothing but "How do you do?" or "I thought perhaps you'd like to have company," and laid on the counterpane a very small tea-rose which was known to have bloomed on a little bush that had been tended like a baby, and brought through the winter only by the greatest care — when Mary Dean did this, it might be thought that she was too wistful and unreviving for a sick-room. Yet many a patient wished more than ever to get well again, if only to do something for this kind nurse in return. They were both useful in their way. It must be confessed that Martha made a great deal the best gruel; but sometimes you wanted one and sometimes the other, and meant no disrespect to the slighted sister.

They lived together on a hilltop just outside the village. The faded yellow story-and-a-half house looked as if it had strayed away a little to be by itself. Perhaps somebody was influenced to build it there so that it would be all ready for Mary Dean, who loved quiet more and more as she grew older. Martha often fretted, and wished that she were in the village. She thought the half a mile a longish walk in bad weather, and was sure they would get more to do if they were right among folks. You would do twenty-five cents' worth yourself many a time rather than rig all up in a rainstorm to lug it up a long hill! If there had been more land with the little house, Martha was sure they could sell it to advantage; but whenever she talked about that, as she would sometimes, in a most fierce way, her sister provoked her a little by not consenting to see the advantage. Mary would only say, "Perhaps you know best," or, "Do you think we could find just the right house?" but she always looked utterly miserable, and brightened up when, after a season of gloomy silence, her more energetic sister would speak about something else. Mary loved every blade of grass on their fifth part of an acre; she loved even the great ledge that took up part of their small domain, and made the rest scorched and dry in midsummer. It seemed to her, if she had to leave the house, that she must give up, not only seeing the sunsets, but the memory of all the sunsets she could remember. The good women were growing old. Martha was rheumatic in cold weather, and it was Martha who went oftenest to the village and upon whom most of the inconvenience came. "I expect to live and die here," she said, one day, to a new customer, who asked them if they had always lived in the old house; "that is, provided I don't die on the road goin' and comin'."

One day, about the middle of November, the sisters were both at home and sat each by her chosen window, stitching busily. Sometimes Mary would stop for a minute or two, and look out across the country, as if she really took pleasure in seeing the leafless trees against the gray sky, and the band of pale yellow in the southwest, the soft pale brown of the fields and pastures, and a bronzed oak here and there against the blackish-green pine woods. Martha thought it a very bleak, miserable sort of day; her window overlooked the road to the village, and hardly anybody had gone by all the afternoon.

"I believe the only thing that would make it worthwhile to live way out here," she said, energetically, "would be a sewing-machine. I could take regular work then from Torby's shop, as some of the folks are goin' to do, and then we could have something to depend upon. You ain't able to go out all weathers, and never was, and 't was all I could do to get through last winter. One time — don't you rec'lect ? — we was shut up here four days, and couldn't have got to the village, to save us, in that big storm. It makes a great difference about the passing since they cut that new cross-road. And I should like to live where I could be reasonably certain of meetin' privileges; it did seem good to go to Friday evenin' meetin' last week when I was to the Ellis's. I can't feel right to go away and leave you alone, and folks ain't likely to want us both to once, as they used to a good deal."

Mary sighed a little. She knew all these arguments well; she knew that what they wanted was steady work at home in winter. They had only a little money in the bank, for, thrifty as they were, they were unfortunate too, and had lost by a railroad failure a few years ago almost all their lifetime's savings. They could not go out to work much longer, Mary knew that well. Martha need not say it over so many times; and she looked up at Martha, and was surprised, as if it were the first time she had ever noticed it, to see that she was almost an old woman. Never quite that! The brisk, red cheeked girl who had been her childish pride and admiration could never be anything else, in spite of the disguises and changes with which time had masked her faded countenance. Martha had a lover, too, in the days of the red cheeks; sometimes Mary wondered at her bravery in being so cheerful and happy; for the elder sister had taken her life as it came, with such resignation and uncomplainingness. Perhaps Mary felt the loss of the lover more than Martha herself, who had suffered at first, but the grief had grown vague years ago. They had not been engaged very long, and she had hardly grown used to her new relationship before his sudden death came. She had often told herself that it was all for the best, and in spite of that liked to have people know that she was not exactly like other unmarried women who never had been urged to change their situation. But when Martha had been sitting in silence, lost in thought, and Mary's tender sympathies had woven many happy dreams for her, she was apt to shatter the dreams at last by some very unsentimental remark about the jacket they were making, or the price of tea. No doubt she often had her own sad thoughts, for all that.

There was just such a silence in this November afternoon, and Mary, as usual, humbly wondered if her sister were lonely and troubled, and if she herself were half so good and tender as she ought to be to one so dear and kind. At last Martha said, in a business-like way: "Next week we shall be getting ready for Thanksgiving. I don't expect we shall do so much as usual; I don't see where the money's comin' from. We had better get along without a chicken, anyways; they're goin' to bring a high price, and ours must pay for the wood as far as they 'll go."

"I'm thankful as I can be every day," said Mary, softly. "I don't know what I should do without you, sister. I hope the Lord won't part us;" and her lip quivered as she spoke. "You thought we never should pull through this year," she resumed, in a more commonplace tone; "but here we are, after all, and we've done well, and been fed, and kept warm."

"The next year we ought to shingle the house and set the fences into some kind of shape. I wish we could sew up things outdoors well's we can in;" and Martha smiled grimly.

"We do, don't we?" and the younger sister laughed outright. "I wish we did have a sewing-machine. I dare say by and by they'll get cheaper. I declare it doesn't seem five years since the war was over."

"There's John Whitefield," said Martha, angrily; and Mary looked frightened. She was always so sorry when this topic was started. "He never gives a thought to what our folks did for him. I shouldn't know him if I was to see him, and we are all the own cousins he's got on his father's side. It does seem as if he might take some interest in us now we're all growing old together. He must have read our names in the list of those that lost in the railroad, and have known 't was all we'd got."

"Perhaps he thinks we don't take any interest in him," ventured Mary, timidly. "I have sometimes thought about him, and wondered if he supposed we were set against him. There was so much hard feelin' between the families when we were all young, and we wouldn't speak to him when we were girls. A young man would be cut by that as much as anything" —

"I wouldn't speak to him now, either," and Martha's voice and her linen thread snapped together. "Everybody said they treated our folks outrageously. You needn't expect me to go meechin' after such thankless and unprincipled creatures."

Mary hardly knew what gave her such courage. "I don't want to vex you, I 'm sure," she said, simply. "If he didn't answer or didn't treat us well any way, I should think as you do; but I should like to ask him to come and spend Thanksgiving Day with us, and show him a forgivin' spirit. He ain't so well off that he need think we've got low motives; and" — taking courage — "you know this'll be the first Thanksgiving since his wife died — if 't was his wife we saw mentioned in the paper."

"I must say you are consistent with our havin' nothin' for dinner," smiled Miss Martha, grimly, clicketing together her big needle and her steel thimble without any top. "I won't lend myself to any such notions, and there's an end to it."

She rose and disappeared angrily into the pantry, and began to assail the pots and pans as if she had to begin the preparations for Thanksgiving at that very moment. But Miss Mary Dean, whom everybody thought a little flighty and unpractical, went on sewing as long as the pale daylight lasted. She did not know why she was so disappointed about not inviting their unknown cousin. She had not thought of him very often; but she had always been a little ashamed and sorry about the family quarrel that had made everybody so bitter and unforgiving when she was a girl. Her father thought that this cousin's father cheated him of his rights in the old home farm.

At least three days afterward Sister Martha was discovered to be very silent and unreasonable; and, in spite of previous experiences, Miss Mary was entirely surprised to be told late in the evening, just as they were going to bed, that a letter had been sent that day to Cousin John asking him to come to spend Thanksgiving with them on the hilltop. "You'd never have been satisfied without it, I suppose," the good woman said, grudgingly, as she went hurrying about the room; and gentle Mary was filled with fear. She knew that it would be a trouble to her sister, and an unwelcome one; but at last she felt very glad, and was aggravatingly grateful as she thanked the head of the family for this generous deed. "I don't know why my heart was so set on it," she announced later, with great humility, and Martha sniffed unmistakably from under the patchwork counterpane. "I hope he won't stop long," she observed, quite cheerfully. And so peace was restored, and Miss

Martha Dean thought about the dinner and talked over her frugal plans, while Mary listened with pleased content, and looked out through the little bedroom window from her pillow to see the white, twinkling, winter-like stars.

"Goodness me!" exclaimed Martha on Thanksgiving morning; "there he comes, and he looks as old as Methusaleh!" The sisters stood together and watched their guest climbing the long hill, and made characteristic comments. "He does look real lonesome," said Mary, but Martha bustled off to look at the chicken which had just been put into the oven. "He looks as if he were hungry," she growled on the way, and took a complacent look into the kettles after she had seen that the oven continued to be in a proper state of warmth. There was enough for her to do to look after the dinner. Mary could attend to the company: but, after all, it was good to have company, especially someone who seemed to be glad to be with them. He had grown to look like her own dear, honest-hearted father in these latter years; he could not be a bad man, and it seemed a great while since they had seen one of their own folks at the table.

So Martha put her whole heart into making her little dinner just as good as it could be. She sat down in the front room once or twice and tried to talk over old times, but she was not very successful; they were constantly running against unpleasant subjects; it seemed as if the mistaken household that had been divided against itself had no traditions of anything but warfare.

But the guest was pathetically glad to come; he could talk to his cousin Mary about the pleasure Martha's note had given him. He did not say that it was not very affectionate, but he told the truth about having often wished since he had grown older that they could talk over the old times and have a kinder feeling toward each other. "And I was so broken up this year," he added, plaintively. "I miss my wife worse and worse. She was some years younger than I, and always seemed so pleasant and sprightly — well, if one of you girls is left without the other, you'll know something about it, that's all I can say," and a sudden pang shot through the listener's heart. And Mary Dean looked so sorry and so kind that she had to listen to a great many things about the wife who had died. Cousin

John Whitefield moved her sympathy more and more, and by the time dinner was ready they were warm friends. Then there was the dinner, and the two elderly women and their guest enjoyed it very much. Miss Martha had put on the best table-cloth and the best dishes. She had done all she could to make the little festival a success, and presently even she was filled with the spirit of the day, and did not let the least shadow of disapproval show itself in her face when Mary said: "Sister, I'm sure we ought to be very thankful today for all these good things and for Cousin John's company. I don't feel as if we ever should make out to be enemies again;" and the cousin shook his head more than once, while something like a tear glistened in the eyes that were turned toward Mary Dean. They talked of old times; they said to each other that they would let bygones be bygones. Some of the sisters' friends had been very kind; one had given them a present of cranberries, which Martha liked very much, but had denied herself, since they were so dear that year.

Cousin John had evidently dressed himself with great care, but he looked untended, and the sisters' shrewd eyes saw where a stitch or two was needed and a button had been lost. It seemed more friendly than ever when he stood before Martha to have his coat mended; it only took a minute. And her eyes were the best, Mary said, proudly.

"Girls," said the old man, suddenly; "girls, I want to know if, with all your sewing trade, you haven't got any sewing-machine?" And the girls looked at each other wistfully, and answered No.

"Now, I know what I'll do for you," and the withered face brightened. "I'm going to send you over Maria's. She set everything by it; 't was one her brother gave her — Josiah, that's so well off in New York. She says 't was one of the best; and there it has stood. I've been thinking I should have to sell it. I'll send it over right away." And he looked from one delighted face to the other. "You won't refuse, now?" he asked; as if there had been any danger of that! And the sisters confessed how puzzled they had been about their winter's work; they had not acknowledged so fully even to each other that some of their old customers had died, that it hardly paid to do hand-sewing, and hardly anybody needed tailors' work, somehow; and they were not able to be out in all weather, or to be of as much service to their neighbors as they used. But they were sure to do well now if they had a machine. Mr. Torby, at the shop, paid excellent prices for the best work.

Cousin John stayed until the next day, and they watched him go down the hill with many feelings of gratitude and respect. "It takes two to make a quarrel, but only one to end it," said Martha, turning suddenly to Mary. They both felt younger than they had for a great while, and they pitied their cousin's aged looks and slow steps. "'T was all owing to you," she went on, in a tone that was not usual with her. "Mary, I believe you've chosen the better part, and you've listened to the Lord's words while I've been cumbered with much serving." But Mary would have it that only Martha could have made Cousin John so comfortable, and got him the good Thanksgiving dinner.

"The dinner's the least part of it," said Martha, this time in her every-day, short fashion of speech. "There! it's beginning to snow. I wish, if there's a good fall of it, we could just put this house on runners and slide down hill!" But she looked very good-natured, and Mary laughed softly.

"You say that every year, don't you, Martha?" said she. "Just think how long we've been wishing for a sewing-machine, and now we're really going to have one. I suppose you'll know just how to use it before it has been here a day."

❦ THE NEWS FROM PETERSHAM ❦

Mrs. PEAK HAD BEEN to Petersham herself, to spend Thanksgiving with her niece, and brought the first account of old Mr. Johnson's illness. Mrs. Jesse Johnson, his daughter-in-law, had come in for a few minutes Thursday afternoon, and had said it was the first time since she could remember that the old gentleman had not been in his seat in church on Thanksgiving Day. And they all felt as if it were a great break.

"He would insist upon setting at the table," said Mrs. Jesse, "but he looked too feeble to be out of his bed. These bad colds take hold of a man of his years."

After the visitor had gone Mrs. Peak and her niece Martha talked a good deal about the changes in the family which would be sure to come when Mr. Johnson died.

"I know that Jesse's folks are depending upon getting a lift," said Martha. "Mis' Jesse has hinted as much to me more than once, for she says Jesse's got more than he can carry in his business, and everything would be easy if he only had a little more capital. Truth is, I have an idea that he's teased a good share away from his father now, and the old gentleman isn't so ready as he used to be to further his projects. And there's William, his other son, I know it to be a fact that he is intending to go out West when his father's taken away. He has had a notion of it for a good while; his wife's sister's folks are all out there and doing well."

"They'll be very much missed as a family," said Mrs. Peak; "how Petersham has changed from what it was when I was a girl!"

When she went home the next day she was quite downhearted, and told Asa Fales, who happened to be at the depot when the train came in and offered to carry her home, that old Mr. Daniel Johnson was breaking up — at least, so his family seemed to think. Asa Fales was deeply concerned; the two villages were only a few miles apart, and he had been a Petersham boy. It was old Mr. Johnson to whom he owed his rise in the world, and he remembered that he might never have owned his flourishing country store if it had not been for this kind friend's assistance. Besides, he had been confident of Mr. Johnson's support if he should make up his mind to buy a large tract of woodland which would pay well for being cleared that very next winter. He was already indebted to him, however, and it would be a very different thing if he were the debtor of the eager heirs. So with all this in his mind he questioned Mrs. Peak anxiously, and they concluded that Mr. Johnson's end was not far distant.

"Of course he made a great effort to get to the table on account of its being Thanksgiving," said Asa, sorrowfully, "but I'm afraid he'll give right up now. I'd ride right over to see him tomorrow, but I can't get away. It's right in my busy time; I'm buying up a great deal of wood this fall, and some of 'em are bringing it in now on wheels instead of waiting for snow."

"The snow does keep off late this year," said Mrs. Peak. "Here it's the first o' December, and there's only been one flurry that was hardly more than a hoar-frost."

They reached the little gray house behind the lilac-bushes, where Mrs. Peak lived alone, and as she unlocked its side-door and went in, it seemed strangely cold and lonely. "I must look about for a likely kitten," she said to herself; "they're a sight of company, and what trouble it gave would be no harm. I declare it makes me feel lonesome; all the folks I have always been used to knowing are a-dying off. I always set a good deal by Daniel Johnson."

Two neighbors looked up the road a little later than this from their kitchen windows, and seeing a light in Mrs. Peak's kitchen also, said to themselves that she might be lonely that evening without anybody to speak to, and they would step over and hear the news. They met at the door, each with a shawl over her head and her knitting-work in her hands, — and were welcomed most heartily. Mrs. West, who was very fond of talking, began at once to describe her experiences Thanksgiving morning, when she found that the cats had stolen into the pantry during the night, and mangled the turkey so that it was only fit to be thrown away. It was too late to get another, except a rack of bones fit only for a lantern, that had been left at Fales's store.

"I didn't know what in the world I should do. There was all the folks coming; his sister and all the child'n, and my brother and his wife, and we three at home are middlin' hearty — but there; we made out with the chicken-pie and a spare-rib I put right in. It so happened I had one that was thawed. An' I took those cats and soused 'em well in a tub o' water, after I'd give 'em as good a beating as I knew how. And after a while they stole in half froze, and set by the stove meek as Moses with their paws tucked underneath 'em, and when I'd look at 'em they'd mew at me both together 'thout making a sound. For all I was so worked up, I had to laugh."

They all laughed again at the cats, while Mrs. Peak acknowledged that she had just been thinking of getting a kitten, but such accounts as this were discouraging, — and Mrs. West promptly offered her own virtuous pussies, which amused the little company very much.

"You haven't told us yet whether you heard anything over at Petersham," said Mrs. Rogers, the other guest, at which Mrs. Peak's face grew long.

"I had a beautiful visit with Martha," she answered, "but I've been feeling anxious to hear again from old Mr. Daniel Johnson. Jesse's wife came in and said he seemed very feeble. He didn't make no effort to get out to meetin' Thanksgivin' Day, and Martha said she'd noticed he looked pale and kind o' wizened up two or three weeks ago."

"I suppose the cold weather pinched him," suggested Mrs. West. "Well, he'll be a great loss."

"I heard from him direct this morning," continued Mrs. Peak, mournfully. "I called to Jesse's oldest boy as he went by, and he said his grand'ther wasn't any better. I asked if he was abed, and he said, 'No.' He's got a sight o' resolution; I shouldn't wonder if he didn't take his bed at all."

"I don't see how they'll pay their minister the salary they give him now, when they lose Mr. Johnson," said Mrs. Rogers. "He's always ready to give, and he does what he can for his folks. I shouldn't wonder if he hadn't but a little property left, after all he's had to do, and being out o' business for some years now."

"He's kept his money a-movin'," observed Mrs. West. "There ain't no such business man about here, but there's been plenty o' hands reached out to take what they could get. Well, 't is all over now; he won't last a great while if he's as feeble as you say. His father went just the same way, only kept the house a week, and his bed the last day."

"I should have gone right over to see him myself yesterday," said the hostess, "but it kept raining steady all day, same as it did here, I suppose."

"They'll be likely to have his funeral from the meeting-house, won't they?" asked Mrs. Rogers, solemnly; but nobody could answer her question.

Next day being Sunday, and most of the congregation coming from the scattered farms, there was the usual exchange of greetings and inquiries for news. And in this way the sad story of Mr. Johnson's last illness was spread far and wide before night. And in passing from one to another, the report became every hour more serious. At last some one ventured to say that, judging from what she had just heard, the poor man could not now be living. And the listener felt justified in announcing that Mrs. Smith thought there was no doubt that he was dead.

Late on Sunday night Mrs. West brought the news to Mrs. Peak.

"He heard it from some one who stopped at Asa Fales's, but there wasn't no particulars;" and Mrs. Peak said nobody had any idea Mr. Johnson would go so soon. It was a great shock to her; as much as if she had not known of his illness.

"Death is always sudden at the last," said Mrs. West. "I suppose you will go over to the funeral? — it seems a pity you should have come home Saturday, don't it?"

"I shall get ready to go by the first train," answered the old lady, crying a little. "I declare I wish I'd gone to the house before I come away. It ain't that I think of the expense of going to Petersham twice, for that's nothing at such a time as this, but I can't feel reconciled to not seeing him again. He was a most amiable Christian man, — there won't be many dry eyes in Petersham the day he's buried. I've known him ever since I've known anybody."

So by the earliest train next day Mrs. Peak went back to Petersham. Her countenance wore a solemn expression. She felt herself to be one of the chief mourners, though her place in the procession would probably be not far from the least afflicted end. As she stepped down from the car, she pulled a very long face, and was surprised to see no signs of the calamity which had befallen the village. She meditated upon the way the world moves on though its best men die, and took her way, to save time, through the back streets to her niece Martha's.

"Well, Martha," she said, sadly, "I'm sure I didn't think I should be back again so soon when I left you. When do they bury?"

"Who?" asked Martha, much amazed. She was busy washing, and was not in the least prepared for her aunt's appearance. She was used to making careful arrangements when she expected guests — being, as her friends said, very set in her ways — and if there was anything she disliked it was a lack of ceremony, even from her nearest relatives.

"I haven't heard of any death," she assured her aunt, who was apparently much perplexed.

"Somebody told the Wests last night that Mr. Dan'el Johnson had passed away, and Mis' West came right out to tell me," Mrs. Peak explained at last.

Martha began to laugh. "He was out to meeting last night as sure as the world," she said. "He's had a bad cold, — you know he's always been subject to fall colds, — but he's about again. I heard Jesse's wife fussin' at him about doin' up his throat when we were comin' out o' the meetin'-house last night."

"She was dreadful down-hearted about him, I'm sure, when she come in Thanksgiving night," ventured Mrs. Peak in self-defense.

"Now, Aunt Peak," said Martha, "haven't you seen enough of Lydia Johnson by this time to know that she always thinks everything and everybody is going to rack and ruin? She was cheerful about the old gentleman to what she is sometimes. To be sure we all know he's getting along in years."

"Seems to me I do rec'lect she is apt to look on the dark side," reflected Mrs. Peak.

"But now, Marthy, don't speak to anyone of what my errand was in coming over. I've got a little shopping any way that I forgot last week, and folks will think we're dreadful hungry for news over our way."

"It does look like it," chuckled Martha. "But do stop to dinner, aunt, now you're over; it's coming winter and you may not get started again. 'T is a pity there ain't something else for you to go to. I s'pose you've heard that story about the old ladies that set out for a funeral and found they'd missed the day, and asked the folks if they didn't know of a funeral they *could* go to?"

"Marthy," said her Aunt Peak, "I should think you had no feelin's. It wasn't my fault as I know of that the story got about. I did speak of it to one or two that his son's wife appeared concerned, and when word come that he was gone I only thought she had good reason to be anxious; and he was an old friend, and a leader in church interests, and I thought, natural enough, I 'd come right over."

"Don't take it hard of me, joking with you," said Martha, "but it is kind of amusing when you come to look at it and see how stories get made up and set going out of nothing. Everyone of 'em thinks they tell the truth, and first thing you know there's a lie traveling about fast as lightning," and she turned to her neglected washing, as if no time must be lost.

"I can't get back before two. I'm sorry I happened to trouble you on an inconvenient day, I'm sure," said Mrs. Peak, humbly. "I'll step down the street for a while and do a few errands, and you mustn't let me put you onto Just a cup of tea and a taste of bread and butter'll be all I ask for," and Martha nodded and told her aunt not to worry, and to have as good a time as she could.

The old lady's pride had met with a sad downfall — she did not know how to face the people at home. But luckily she was saved the first acknowledgment, as Asa Fales had reached Petersham before her and had found Mr. Daniel Johnson briskly at work by the garden trellis covering his grape-vines.

He had prudently avoided any reference to the next world, and, indeed, had learned the falseness of the story from a Petersham man whom he had met on the road. So he entered at once upon the project of buying the pine woods between Gay town and Hollis, and found to his great satisfaction that his old friend would be glad to join him if the affair could be well arranged.

Mrs. Peak herself met Mr. Johnson, and could hardly look him in the face when she asked for his health. And when the neighbors came in one after another that evening after she was again comfortably established at home, she said, "You may laugh at me all you have a mind to, but I don't mean to need another lesson like this. I think it's a good deal better to mind what we've got to do instead of livin' on what folks have got to say; but it's hard to teach an old dog new tricks, and I suppose I shall always like to hear what news there is a-goin'."

🙚 THE TWO BROWNS 🙚

Part I.

BROWN LEFT HIS CHAIR by the fire somewhat impatiently, and dropped his newspaper on the rug; he crossed the dining-room to the bay-window, and stood with his back to his wife, looking out at the weather. Women were such persistent geese! He had a vague idea that she might take some notice of the disagreeable sleet and wind, and relent a little about hinting that he had better be at his office. She had already asked him to renew her subscription to the church newspaper (he would have to leave the stage and walk a block and a half), and had said that he must look in at her brother Bob's counting-room some time during the day to ask for his wife's health. She had furthermore given him two letters to post, and had reminded him three times that he must not forget them.

"I believe that I will not go to the office today," Brown announced presently, with considerable dignity and even sternness, as if he would not brook the idea of being contradicted in any shape. His wife said nothing to this, which was a great disappointment; and after growing more and more disturbed for a minute or two he turned and offered his explanations. Mrs. Brown was devoting herself to the baby, while the nursery-maid was busy upstairs in the baby's luxurious quarters. Brown was usually neither too proud nor too much occupied to devote himself to his daughter, also, but now he walked stiffly back to the big chair by the fire, and took no notice of the little hands that were put out to him. The baby's mother flushed suddenly with something like anger, very unusual in her gentle face.

"It is such an abominable day," said Brown. "I don't feel very energetic. There won't be a soul inside the office door, unless it's a book agent. I am going to make myself comfortable at home, and see something of you and — yes, you little pink!"

He had come, so near to neglecting the baby that his better nature could submit no longer, and he caught the smiling child, and went prancing round the breakfast table until she shrieked with delight, and family harmony was restored. Mrs. Brown smiled, too, — they were a happy household; but she looked serious again directly, and returned to the charge.

"Ben, dear," she said, "I don't like to have you neglect your profession."

Brown stopped his capering, and the cups and plates gave a final jingle. "When you know perfectly well how it neglects me!" he responded solemnly, with a twinkling eye.

Even in the presence of the baby Mrs. Brown did not like to have such confessions made, and she looked up reproachfully. She kept up with great care the fiction of her husband's having already a fair law practice for a young man of his age, and a very promising outlook. Brown had no imagination; he made no complaint; he knew plenty of fellows in the same box, and was not going to shoulder the whole shame of paying rent for a clientless office. He had begun to get tired of spending his days there altogether, even with the resource of taking all the time he liked for an elaborate and social luncheon. His wife had been growing a trifle anxious lately because it was so difficult to tempt his appetite at dinner-time, and Gales, the wit of the luncheon club, had said in his affected little drawling voice only the day before, "Shall have to cut this sort of thing, you know; getting too stout, and always hated eating my dinner in the middle of the day. Could do it with one client, but tomorrow I'm expecting another." Brown suddenly remembered this, and smiled, because he had a quick, amusing fear lest the bad weather might keep Gales's client at home. Then he gave a sigh, and gently deposited the baby in her mother's lap. "I will go, you hard-hearted monsters," he said, kissing them both, "but why I ever let myself be coaxed into studying law is the puzzle of my life. If I had something to do I would work like a beaver. I've got it in me, fast enough, but I hate this make-believe business. So would you."

"I do feel sorry about it; you know I do," answered Lucy, with great tenderness and sympathy. "I should be perfectly unhappy. But you have your studies, Ben, dear."

"I begin to hate those old yellow books," said Ben. "Now, if my father had let me study engineering, as I wished, I should have been in the middle of things by this time."

"You never would have broken the chain?" asked Lucy, with unfeigned anxiety roused by such treason. She had been so proud of Brown's being the fourth lawyer of his line and of his precocious scholarship. He was only twenty-eight years and two months old at that moment, beside, and it was much too soon to lose all hope about his future.

Brown went manfully out into the sleet a few minutes later, and his wife and the baby watched him from the window. He was a handsome, good-natured young man, and it was impossible not to be proud of him; or to feel sorry at his temporary discomfort as he slipped and plodded along the encumbered sidewalk. When he had paused for a moment at the corner to throw a last kiss to the baby and wave his hand, old Mr. Grandison, who stood at his own window opposite, nodded his head in sage approval. "Good fellow," he grumbled, with his chin plunged deep in his old-fashioned black silk stock. "Comes of a good family, and is sharp after his business." The damp air blew in at the window, and the spectator of Brown's departure was obliged to turn away and seek his fireside again. He would have been perfectly thankful to change places with the young man, and go down town to do a stiff day's work, as he used twenty years ago.

Lucy Brown had turned aside from her window, also, and begun an eager morning's work. She had been dreadfully afraid that Ben would insist upon staying at home, and she felt hard-hearted in very truth. But when she had waked up that morning to find it snowing, she had resolved to have the books in the library thoroughly cleaned. Nobody would come in, and she would muster the household force, and of course attend to Ben's private desk and papers herself. She was still excited by her narrow escape from complete disappointment, but she hoped she had not seemed anything but kind and affectionate in urging her husband that day of all others to go to his office.

Mr. John Benedict Brown had an uneventful journey to his place of business. He liked the bad weather, on the whole, — he had so few things ordinarily to match his youthful energy against, — and he met two or three companions in misery, if one had any right to call these briefless barristers by such a hard name. Each carried his green bag, but Brown's friend Gales unconsciously held his in such a way that the shape of a box of cigars was displayed unmistakably as its only contents. Gales's office was farther down the street, and Brown remembered his promise about the subscription just in time not to pass the office of the paper. He would have sent a note to the publisher, to do his errand, but Lucy was very strenuous upon his settling the matter in person. She had paid for a year in advance, and the bill had been rendered again. She was most dependent upon this particular publication, and seemed absurdly anxious to stand well in the publisher's estimation. There was only one other man in the office beside the clerk, when Brown entered. This other man stood with his back to the door, looking over a file of newspapers, and until the small matter was settled, in a general and impersonal fashion that would have wounded Mrs. Brown, he gave no sign of consciousness of Brown's presence.

Then he laid down the newspapers and approached our friend. "Snooks, old boy, how are you?" he inquired affectionately, and a little timidly, too, as if not quite certain of his reception.

The very name of Snooks was sufficient; it had been Brown's nickname at the school where he had fitted for college. Anybody who called him Snooks had a right to favor after the space of at least a dozen years since those happy days when he had heard it often. This schoolmate had not followed the class to college, but he had been a good crony in his day, and a lad of some cleverness and an erratic habit of mind. Only a few days before, Gales, who had also been at the school, had asked our hero what had become of Checkley. Old Shekels they used to call him, for the inconsequent reason that he never had two cents in his pocket. He was kept at his studies by some kind and charitable friend, who forgot to an aggravating extent to supply the minor comforts of life. Checkley had developed an amazing gift for maintaining himself by an ingenious system of barter, like those savages who have not got so far in civilization as any sort of exchequer or strictly financial arrangements.

The old brotherliness of the past quickly filled Brown's heart. Checkley looked hungry, as usual, but he would take him to the office and make him a welcome companion that dull morning, and by and by they would have a bit of luncheon together. After all, the day promised well; he had feared a very special lack of entertainment.

"Come round to my office," said Brown, warmly. "I've nothing in the world to do this morning. Tell me what you have been about all this time. I'll send for Gales presently; he was asking for you a day or two ago. We're both in the law; lots of time to call our own, too," he added, with a cheerful honesty which his wife would have inwardly lamented and tried to explain.

Checkley was out that day protected by a melancholy fall overcoat and no umbrella, but he took Brown's umbrella, and carried it over both their heads with careful impartiality, as if it were his own. He looked as if he were growing old, which seemed premature in a man of thirty. Brown could not help a suspicion that Checkley had made himself up for some secret purpose. He always used to say that he meant to be a detective, and had been considered immensely clever in some boyish plays and pantomimes. However, another stolen glance made Brown feel certain that this appearance was Checkley as Himself, An Unsuccessful Man, and that the gray hairs which sprinkled his thin, straight, brownish hair were quite genuine. The thinness and lankness of his boyhood had never fulfilled their promise of a robust frame, but appeared to have suffered from exposure and neglect, like an unfinished building which has had time to let its timbers get rain-blackened and look poor.

But the same spirit and shrewd determination twinkled from Checkley's eyes, and he kept step manfully with his well-clothed and well-fed acquaintance. This was a most fortunate meeting. Nothing had ever played better into his hands. Snooks Brown was always a good fellow, and luck was sure to turn.

"You aren't in the *Parishioner's War-Cry* office as a permanent thing, I imagine?" asked Brown, with friendly desire to keep up the conversation, just as they stepped into the elevator. "Odd that we should have happened to find each other there. I never was inside that place before."

"No," said Checkley. "Truth is, it looked quiet and secluded, and I put into harbor there to dry off a little and get my wits together. Temporary asylum. I was paying that clerk the compliment of looking over his newspapers, but I think he was just beginning to suspect that I held them upside down. I had a kind of revenge on him when you came in. It looked as if we had an appointment, you know, and you were always so thundering respectable."

Brown laughed with unaffected pleasure. He was not so far from boyhood as a stranger might imagine. There was something delightful about Checkley's turning up that wet February morning, and telling the most mortifying facts about himself with honest sincerity. He took the wet, thin overcoat and put it away with his own, and would have insisted upon his guest's occupying the best chair in the office, if he had not promptly taken it without any invitation. There was an open wood fire, and Checkley stretched out a pair of very shabby shoes to dry with an air of comfort and satisfaction. He was a schemer, a dreamer, a curious plotter of insignificant things, but he never had been a toady or a beggar, and there was a golden thread of good humor and unselfishness through his unprofitable character.

Brown had taken up a not very ponderous mail that lay on his desk, — two or three bills, as many circulars, and an invitation to make further subscription to the Art Club. He gravely looked these over, and put them in an orderly heap at the further edge of the blotter. Old Shekels's shoes were beginning to steam at the toes, and his host noticed that they looked about the size of his own shoes. At any rate, there was an extra pair of arctics in the office closet that could be offered before they went out to luncheon. Brown felt a glow of kind-heartedness spread itself over him, as he resolved to dress Checkley in comfortable fashion before they parted again. "You look just as you did when we used to stay up after hours, and sit before the fire and tell stories," he said, jovially, to his guest. "I dare say you could spin as good a midnight yarn as ever."

"You rich fellows see the world from a different angle," responded Checkley, who grew more luxurious every moment. "Now it really makes no difference how long you have to wait for practice; it's sure to come, if only when you begin to settle up the family estates. There are half a dozen good round ones; and they never would like to choose anyone else, all those good old aunties of yours. If you had been out of school when your father died, you would have gone on with at least a third of his business, and that was enough for you to handle. It is only a question of time, and you're rich any way. I don't like to see all your first-rate abilities rusting out, nevertheless. I always said there was more good stuff in you than in any of the fellows, — more hold on and push too, if you had anything to push, and got your energy well roused. I should just like to see you in a Western railroad office, making things spin. Now a poor dog like me, thrown out neck and heels into the water to' get to land as best I can by myself, — why, it's a good thing to meet a floating plank to rest a paw on now and then;" and he turned to look Brown full in the eyes with a plaintive, doglike appeal, as if he unconsciously identified himself with his figure of speech.

"What have you been doing, old boy? Can't I lend you a hand, somehow?" asked the sympathetic host. He began to feel that the minus Shekels was driving at something definite, and he did not believe that he should make a fool of himself; but this was the first time that one of his boyhood friends had turned up looking as if the world had used him badly. There ought to be something done about it.

"Look here," said Checkley, with an air of secrecy; and he held out a sheaf of papers, which were produced from his breast-pocket as if the hand well knew its way to them. "I dare say," the owner remarked proudly, "that you wouldn't believe that there is an enormous fortune in that small space?"

Brown tried to look interested, but his doubtfulness showed through.

"It is the surest thing alive," continued Checkley. "Have you got ten thousand dollars you could put your hand on?"

The listener nodded slowly; to tell the truth, he had a little more than that lying idle in the bank, because he really did not know how to reinvest it. The bulk of his property was in the hands of trustees to whom his father had consigned it, but this was some money that had been left him by an old relative, long ago, in his own right. He had a vague idea of putting it into a country-place, some day or other. He had a sentiment about keeping it by itself, and he wanted a nice old-fashioned farm by and by. For the present he and his wife spent their summers with Lucy's mother, who would also have been alone in her great house at Newport. He could say neither yes nor no to such a question, or rather such a questioner, as this; yet a curiosity took possession of him to hear more, and Checkley saw his advantage.

"Now, my boy," he said, pulling his big chair close to Brown's side at the desk, "I helped work this out, and I twisted things round so that I have the right in my own hands. I simply haven't a cent, and I don't know where I can get it, unless you give it to me, to carry out the thing one step more. I need capital," he ended persuasively, and gave another doglike look at Brown.

The situation was growing commonplace. Brown felt for the first time a little bored, and began to wonder how he should get out of it. He also noticed that Old Shekels had singed those confounded old shoes of his. It was becoming doubtful if the arctic overshoes and the luncheon even would be considered a handsome conclusion to their renewed acquaintance.

"Now look here," said Shekels, with a cheerful smile. "You are thinking how you can ever get rid of me, and that you have heard this sort of story before. I'll tell you the rest of it in fifteen minutes, and then you can say that your business claims your time, and I'll disappear like the juggler's rabbit in the hat."

"In the shoes," Brown mentally corrected him, and tried to look resigned, and even pleased; but he played impatiently with his paper-knife. He felt provokingly young and helpless in Checkley's hands.

Brown's legal ancestry and the traditions of his education had not prevented the love of his profession from being largely an acquired taste. He was equal to being a good lawyer by and by, but his head was naturally fitted for affairs; and if there was one thing that he understood more easily than another, it was mechanical intricacies. Checkley did not use his whole fifteen minutes in making sure of this ally.

"I do see it. Do you take me for a blind man?" exclaimed the listener, springing to his feet, and marching across to the window, where he stood with his back to Checkley, just as he had looked out at the storm once before that day. "It is a great temptation, but I can't throw up my law prospects. My career is cut out for me already. But I'll give you a lift, Old Shekels, — hang me if I don't!"

Checkley grew calm as his friend became excited. "Nonsense," said he. "I don't want much of your time; it's your money I'm after. You can keep your law business going, — all the better for you. We are likely to have suits, but nobody can touch us. I don't ask you to decide now. Think it over, and think me over. I've no security to give you but my plan itself."

"Do you smoke?" inquired Brown, amicably, and Checkley answered that he did.

As the story of this day cannot be suffered to grow any longer, the reader must be content to know that these former schoolmates passed a most agreeable morning, that they had a capital luncheon together, — early, lest Checkley might not have breakfasted well, — and that Checkley accepted the overshoes and all other favors with generous lack of protest or false shame.

Part II.

A year from the time when he met his old playfellow, Brown was inclined to repent his whole indulgence in affectionate civilities to a roving schemer. He assured himself that it had been an expensive lesson, but one that he probably needed. A year later Brown was triumphant, and began to flatter himself that he knew a man and likewise a promising enterprise when he saw them. He was doing very well in his law business. The family reputation for clearness of legal vision and successful pleading was gaining new laurels, and young J. Benedict Brown was everywhere spoken of as the most promising man of his age at the New York bar. Detractors hinted that there were dozens of brighter men, but that nobody could help picking up some crumbs of business with such a father and grandfathers behind him. Mrs. Brown led the company of her husband's admirers, and already indulged in dreams of his appearance in the gloomy but noble garb of a chief justice. He was very busy in these days; long ago he had been obliged to take his breakfast at eight o'clock instead of half-past nine, and he was rarely at home until after six o'clock at night, while it was not uncommon that their seven o'clock dinner was considerably delayed. Lucy watched him with increasing anxiety, for fear that he would break himself down with overwork, but he never had seemed in such good health and spirits. The year before he had been so gloomy and despondent for a few weeks that she was always fearing a return, but at present there was no sign of any. To outward view the Benedict Browns were the most prosperous young people in the city. Fortune, position, everything that the social heart desired, seemed to be heaped upon them. A few croaking voices had begun to figure Brown's probable expenses, and to insinuate that he must be living a good way beyond his income. Brown did not look like a debtor, however; he had an older and more determined appearance, as if he had weighty affairs on his mind and a high principle of conduct in regard to them.

One morning early in March the hero of this tale hurried away from his breakfast table, with a quick kiss on the top of his three-year-old daughter's curly warm little head. They had been breakfasting alone together in a delightfully social way, and before Brown put on his overcoat he ran upstairs, two steps at a time, to give another kiss to his wife and a young son some three weeks of age. Mrs. Brown already spoke of the unconscious morsel of humanity with proud respect as Benedict, but Brown himself was provokingly fond of calling him Johnny. He appeared to have a secret satisfaction and deep sense of pride and amusement in denying his son the family name. Who knew whether this might not be the most illustrious of all the five Benedict Browns? At present he was a very important and welcome person indeed in his own family.

"I am in an uncommon hurry this morning," said the father, turning back for one word more as he went out. "I have a business meeting to go to at nine."

Lucy was one of those delightful women who rarely demand particular explanations and are contented with general assurances, and she kindly advised Brown not to get too tired, and to be sure to come home by half-past five if he could; she missed him so much more now that she was not busy herself and had to spend the whole day upstairs. She had a vague desire to know about her husband's business, — it seemed to interest him so much; but she did not like to expose her total ignorance of affairs, and had a theory, besides, that it was better for Ben to shake off his cares when he was at home.

As Ben went down-stairs again, he was attacked by a sense of guilt more uncomfortable than usual, and said to himself that he must really tell Lucy all about the Planter Company. There was no fear of any catastrophe, it was far beyond the realm of experiments, and she was sure to hear of it from somebody else, and to feel hurt at his silence. The wonder was that he had hidden his head in the sand of his first name so long.

The office of J. Benedict Brown, counselor at law, was unvisited, except by its faithful clerk and copyist, until some three hours later in the day. When the young lawyer reached a certain point on Broadway, he turned quickly to the right and went down a side street, as if he were well accustomed to such a course, and knew the shortest cut toward a dingy brick building which bore a clamorous sort of sign, "The Farmer's Right-Hand Man: The Electric Automatic Potato Planter. Brown & Checkley, Manufacturers." The doorway was blockaded with large packing-cases, and, early as it still was for the business world, there were several men in the counting-room, toward which Brown went at once. The workmen near by gave our friend a cheerful morning greeting, and Mr. Checkley, who sat behind his desk, rose soberly, and presented the new-comer to the counting-room audience as "Our head of the firm, gentlemen, Mr. John B. Brown; and now we will proceed to business at once." Brown established himself at another desk, well stocked with papers, and began to hunt for something in a lower drawer, the key of which he had taken from his own pocket. This was evidently not an occasional thing, this business interview; he took on, even to the most indifferent observer's eye, an air of relationship to the place.

"The only thing that seems to be imperative this morning, Mr. Brown," said Checkley, placidly, in a voice directed to the other listeners, "is a decision on our part in regard to the increase of our circular, almanac, and agent departments. We came to no conclusion yesterday. You have the figures before you on that sheet of blue paper. I think the least increase that we can manage is to quadruple the number of circulars and almanacs over that of last year."

Checkley was in the habit of trying to give casual strangers as large an idea as possible of the magnitude of the Planter Company's business, so Brown listened respectfully, and waited for further information.

"These gentlemen," continued Mr. Checkley, "are ready with an offer to make an extensive additional contract for the wood-work of the machines, and we will listen to them. In our liability to meet extraordinary orders at short notice, we are of course obliged to defend ourselves against any possible inability of theirs to furnish supplies. We find that the business grows with such rapidity that it is most difficult to make provision against surprise. You can easily understand" (addressing the small audience) "that an article like ours is invaluable to every man who cultivates over three acres of land. Indispensable, may say, since it saves the hiring of labor, saves time, and saves strength. Such an article is one no farmer will be without when he once sees it work."

Checkley was unusually fluent of speech this morning, and the interview went on prosperously. Somehow, the familiar place and familiar arguments struck Brown with a fresh vividness and air of reality. His thoughts wandered away to his law business for a few minutes, and then he found himself again listening to another account of the electric automatic potato planter which Checkley was giving to a new-comer, a Western man, who was evidently a large dealer in agricultural supplies. There was a row of clerks behind a screen, and their pens were scratching diligently. Brown could see the high stacks of almanacs through the dusty glass walls that fenced the counting-room, — bright red almanacs, which combined a good selection of family reading with meteorological statistics and the praises of the potato planter judiciously arranged on every page. It looked as if there were almanacs enough already for every man, woman, and child in America, but Checkley knew what he was about. Brown had thought that almanacs were a step too low; he was conscious of a shameful wish now and then that he had embarked on any sort of business rather than a patent potato planter. The pride of the J. Benedict Browns, judges and famous pleaders at the bar, had revolted more than once in the beginning against such a sordid enterprise. But as for John B. Brown, this enterprising manufacturer and distributor of an article that no farmer could do without, he felt an increasing pride in his success. He had merely made use of a little capital that was lying idle, and his own superfluous and unemployed energy. He believed that his legal affairs had been helped rather than hindered by this side issue of his, and he and Checkley had fought some amazing fights with the world in the course of their short but successful alliance. Brown lazily opened a directory near at hand, and looked among the B's. It was a new copy, and he nearly laughed aloud at the discovery that he figured twice on the page: Brown, J. Benedict lawyer, Broadway; h. 38th St., and Brown, John B., B. & Checkley machinists, 9th Ave; h. Jersey City. Here was a general masquerade! Checkley lived in Jersey City, and one of the clerks must have given wrong information, or else the directory agent had confused what was told him. Nobody knew where he lived, very likely. They called him The Boss, in the establishment, because he dressed well and had a less brotherly and companionable manner than Checkley. It was surprising, the way a man could hide himself in such a huge city as this. Yes, he must certainly tell Lucy that very night. They would have a capital laugh over it, and he could tease her about making Johnny a partner instead of the fifth at the bar. Lucy was very fond of a joke, and she had no idea how rich they were going to be if affairs went on at this pace. Brown had felt very dishonest for a long time whenever he saw their advertisements in the papers, and had been nearly ready to confess and be forgiven once the summer before, when he and Lucy took a little journey together up the Connecticut River, and Lucy had writhed in contemptuous agony over Checkley's desecration of natural scenery. "Use Brown & Checkley's Electric Automatic Potato Planter, and Save Ten Years of Life," was displayed on rocks and fences everywhere. Checkley himself had used his short summer holiday in leading a gang of letterers into the rural districts, and this was the result. Could a man of ordinary courage confess at such a moment that the name of Brown was in reality her own property, and that she was unconsciously responsible for such vandalism?

Checkley was rushing things this morning; he eagerly assured his guest that they had made the planter pay her own bills after the first six months, and had advertised only as fast as they gained the means. It was the first application of electricity to farming. "Brown and I had little capital to start with, but we knew we had hold of a sure thing. I am not sure that there is anything that corresponds to it in the world of inventions," Checkley continued proudly. "I have been an inventor all my life. Here you have a light-wheeled vehicle that one horse can drag all day and an intelligent child can control. You only need to plow and harrow and manure your ground: then the planter is driven to and fro;

it stops itself at proper distances, a revolving harrow loosens the ground within a space twelve inches in diameter, this harrow is drawn up, the shovel throws the earth out at one side, the hopper lets fall sufficient seed, a second shovel arrangement covers it in, and a weight falls twice and banks it down, the horse steps on between the furrows. My dear sir, in the time I have consumed in telling you, four hills of potatoes are planted as well as if you had done each one separately with your own hoe; the average time is only three-fifths of a minute. A horse soon learns the trick, for the brake is self-acting and stops him in the proper place. The only thing that troubled us in the beginning was the complaint of patrons that the horses gave trouble, and the hills went zigzagging all over the field. This new improvement makes a field as regular as a checker-board. With the brake that stops the planter instantly, the horse learns to anticipate, and makes his four steps forward and stops of his own accord. It is less fatiguing for the horse than a plow or harrow, and a treadmill is barbarous beside it. Then think of the heat of planting time and the waste of human energy! We are now perfecting a rehoer and digger, but our present enterprise is more than we can handle with ease. You have, no doubt, read our testimonials. Hear this: a ten-acre field planted in half a day, with some help from a neighbor, — read for yourself, sir!

"You need to be very careful of the gauges and setting your brakes properly," Checkley confided honestly. "Electricity is a terrible force; there has been one bad accident through such carelessness. The shovel arrangement was not set as it should be, and the machine went on digging straight down, and would have carried the horse with it, if the harness hadn't been so old that he freed himself, and scrambled out of the pit. My dear sir, this will show you the power of that machine; it went down forty feet, right through gravel, rotten rock, and everything, until it struck a solid ledge, and that stopped it at last. The whole neighborhood collected, and they got alarmed, — thought she might be boring for a volcano or something; and they rolled a big boulder out of a pasture near by, and let it drop right down on the planter; but that only damaged the wood-work and partly disabled the running-work, for she kept tossing up splinters for a day or two. The man hadn't a word to say, for it was a springy field, and the planter had struck water somewhere and made him a first-rate well. He had been intending to dig one thereabouts for a good while."

"I want to know!" exclaimed the wide-eyed listener. Brown heard this flow of Checkley's eloquence, and was amused at the response. It seemed that the listener, a worthy, well-to-do Connecticut farmer, had an idea of introducing the automatic potato planter to his neighborhood, and was trying to obtain one on trial at reduced price, with a promise of wide influence in its behalf and cordial recommendation. Checkley believed in favoring the farmers, and the affair was presently concluded. Brown was amazed to hear his companion say that he, Brown, had been thinking that he should like to pay a visit to that neighborhood at county-fair time, and speak to the folks on agricultural topics. Checkley liked his jokes, and Brown smiled, but he turned a little cold, and wondered if they were not going a trifle too fast. There might not be enough of him for two Browns, at this rate! But it was something to find himself a busy, prosperous man instead of an idle, overgrown boy, and among the new firms of its class none stood better than Brown & Checkley.

There was little time left for serious business conference, but Checkley had great executive ability, and so had Mr. John B. Brown of Jersey City, for that matter. Checkley was thin yet and not very well dressed, but he had a buoyant, confident air. "How well he knows human nature, and what a good fellow he is!" thought Brown as they parted. "Snooks is more of a man than the dandy I met in that newspaper office," reflected Checkley. "I never have lost a cent for him, either, but hang me if we haven't had some narrow escapes. I got him in pretty deep once, when he had the worst doubts of me he ever had. Snooks looked solemn, but he never flung at me, or did anything but shoulder half the blame and the worry, like a man."

In the neighborhood of the company's office Brown met several business acquaintances, who gave him a friendly good-morning. He had gathered a whole new circle of associates, in his character of senior partner of Brown & Checkley. He had indulged in bad lunches with these friends, and already figured largely in the agricultural-implement world; he would have been deeply gratified if he had heard somebody say, as he went by, "That's Brown, of the Planter Company. Those fellows are sweeping everything before them this spring. They've got hold of as big a thing as the McCormick reaper."

It was ten or fifteen minutes' walk between the two offices, and when J. Benedict Brown, Esq., seated himself at his desk he was still thinking about his other business, which he usually insisted upon putting out of his mind. He never had looked at it so entirely from the outside. He was at heart a most conservative person. He was more fettered than he knew by his family pride and traditions, and he had become persuaded of his ability to follow the law in a way that he never used to expect. He felt it in him to make his influence recognized at the bar, and to handle heavy pieces of business. Now that Checkley was so well established he could slip out, and hold only a silent partnership, if he pleased. Yet an opposing judgment in his own mind at the moment prevented him from cordially accepting such an idea. There were some things, and he knew it, that Checkley could not have planned nor have carried without him, and the concern might easily fall to pieces even now. There was his own boy, however, who must inherit as fair a name from him as he had from his father. There had never yet been a dishonored man of his name. Checkley had counted upon the value of the family reputation at first; he insisted that they were throwing away a great advantage by not adding the prefix of J. Benedict to the plain Brown & Checkley. J. Benedict Brown was a name of historical renown. Checkley did not begin to understand yet that John B. Brown was as utterly unknown to the friends of the J. Benedict Browns as if he and his potato planter had never existed. He simply knew that Snooks was old-maidishly eager to keep his two occupations apart, and that only from half-past eight to ten and from three o'clock until dinner-time he was the steady shaft-horse of Brown & Checkley.

Brown sat in the Broadway office, busy at his work, having finished his reflections without coming to any new decisions. He was working up a law case that he took great pride in. All his inherited cleverness and a new love for such a puzzle delighted him; he never had felt a keener sense of his own power, and the planter was utterly forgotten.

Someone entered the office, and gave a chair one aggressive pull across the polished wood floor. It sounded as if the caster had left a damaging scratch, and Brown looked round with not a little annoyance. He felt a strange suspicion that one of his Planter Company associates had at last hunted him down. There was an inner room for purposes of private consultation, and Brown signified, after a proper interval, that the stranger might go there. It was a darkish place, where he had once tried to have his own desk; but it was much too gloomy, especially in the days when there was nothing to do. Except when he was at court, or at his other business, he was very faithful to his post, and the stranger need not have been so uureasonably glad to find him at his office.

"I see that you're your father's own son," the client began, in an asthmatic voice. He looked like a cross old fellow, and Brown had an instant sense of relief because the first words had not been suggestive of the other place of business. "I knew your father and grandfather before you," said Mr. Grandison, "and I've been out of lawyers' hands these twenty years, more or less; but I've got some fight left, and when I got my blood up yesterday about some infringements, I thought over to whom I could give the case, and I decided that I would come round and look you over, to see if I could trust you with such a piece of work. I don't know whether you're not too young now, but it'll be a feather for you if you can handle it. I'm ready to pay what the work's worth, — I'll tell you that to begin with."

The word "infringements" had an unpleasant sound, but Brown waited patiently. He had some knowledge of the man, for whom his father had gained a famous case. Grandison was an inventor. On the whole, he could recall the case perfectly; he had tried to make himself, familiar with it, for future use; but there was no possibility of those questions being reopened.

"My factories go on like clock-work, and have these thirty years," said the old man. Brown began to feel a personal dislike. "I thought I had disposed of all opponents and rivals long ago. Jenks and Rowley are our regular lawyers, but now they're getting old, and they don't own me, any way. You see there are a couple of jackasses, over on Ninth Avenue, who have started up an electric potato planter, — a capital good thing it is, too, — that runs so close to that cog-wheel arrangement in the steam harrow we make that I'm going to stop them short, if I can; or, if I can't do that, I'll buy 'em out, if it costs a million to do it. You can't afford to let such a business as mine scatter itself, and I mean to hold it together as long as I am here to do it."

Brown felt a dampness gather on his forehead; then his manhood arose triumphant, and his courage declared itself equal to this emergency. He was not caught stealing, neither had he done anything dishonorable. There was no real incongruity in a Benedict Brown's being interested in a potato planter; it had all been a fair, above-board business. He was ready to stand up for it.

"I've been living in Thirty-Eighth Street," said the client, "and I have often watched you come and go. I like to see a lad diligent and right after his business, as you are, and ready to go down town an hour or two earlier in the morning than the fashion is. I've had my eye on you for a year or two. I started in life a poor boy, and never had the backing up that was ready for you; but I keep the run of my affairs, I can tell you. I don't get down town every day, by any means, but a thing like this that I want to consult you about fires me all up."

"Will you give me an idea of the case, Mr. Grandison?" asked Brown, politely. He was afraid he might be taking an unfair advantage, but the words were out, and the old manufacturer, with much detail, laid the grievance before him.

"They're smart young men," he ended. "I don't know their match. I hear they had a small capital, and laid it out mostly in advertising. One of them got hold of a half-worked-out notion and completed it, and bought out the owner's right; and there was a small manufactory over in Jersey that had been swamped, and they got that for a song, too; and the minute the machine was on the market it went like wildfire. In spite of constant extensions, they have been able to meet their obligations right along. I don't want to harm 'em if they'll treat me fairly. I'll give 'em a handsome sum down to sell out quietly, or I'll fight 'em all to pieces."

"Perhaps they can stand a fight, and can prove that their machine is no infringement on anybody's," suggested the lawyer, with a good deal of spirit.

Mr. Grandison gave him a shrewd glance. "This Brown is no relation to you, I hope?" he said, doubtfully; but Brown flushed quickly, and made a little joke about the name's not being at all uncommon. The client thought he was not pleased at being associated with a firm of machinists, and was sorry he had spoken. The boy felt older than he looked, no doubt.

When the interview was ended, Brown, who had been very inexpressive of his opinions all the way through, assured his visitor that there were some reasons why he would not give any answer then about undertaking the case, and would ask his leave to defer a direct reply until the next day. "I shall be very glad to stop as I go up town in the afternoon," said our friend. The elder man thanked him, and said he should count it a great favor, if the weather were no better than at present, and went limping away. Poor old soul! it was late for him to be taking pleasure in quarrels with his fellow-men.

Checkley was going over to the works that afternoon, and there was no hope of seeing him until the next morning, so Brown gave all his mind that he possibly could to being J. Benedict, the rising lawyer. He had some perplexing business upon which he tried hard to fix his attention, but the affairs of John B. Brown and the potato planter kept rising before him in an uneasy, ghostlike way that was most disagreeable. He had put more of his thoughts into those side interests than he had been aware. The two years had gone by like a dream, but they had left a good many permanent evidences of their presence. There was one of the teamsters, who had broken his leg early in the winter, and whom Brown had visited in the hospital, besides looking after the patient's family. He had built up his own business reputation, and had grown ambitious about the success of the firm. He had determined at first to say nothing, even to his wife, until he knew whether he had made a fool of himself or not, but he was perfectly aware now that he had not made a fool of himself. He was evolving plans for giving all their workmen some share in the business, and was increasingly glad that he had a chance to work out some experiments in the puzzling social questions of the day. He was ready now to be something of a statesman. He was willing to believe that he had got hold of the right thread of the snarled skein that linked labor with capital. His wife knew that he had some business interests apart from his law reports and his practice, and none of his friends would be surprised that he had been speculating a little. Gales would have got at the whole story, and told it, too; but he had gone abroad months before, and relinquished his profession altogether, for the time being. Perhaps the time had come to choose between the two Browns; it would be hard to play both characters, if the cares of either should double, for instance, and he was, perhaps, fated to be J. Benedict, after all. This was a melancholy thought, and the old wish returned that his other enterprise had concerned anything but an automatic potato planter. It might give him a nickname, and he never would be able to live the silly story down. Checkley was sure to project something new, and yet he was truly proud of the firm of Brown & Checkley, and would not see it cheated.

Next day, Checkley happened to be alone in the office, and his partner beckoned him out into an empty corner of their place of business, where they were well removed from the clerks and their scratching pens. Checkley laughed and shouted, and was at first unable to give any answer. "Wants you to bring a suit of infringement against yourself, does he?" he gasped at length. "Go ahead, my boy; nobody'll know the difference. It will advertise us enormously. I have told you a dozen times that nothing would do us so much good as a rousing lawsuit. Now don't put on your best J. Benedict manners, but listen to me. I'm not going to work myself to death. We have laid by something handsome already; if the old fellow will add to it, I am perfectly willing to sell out, if you are, just to make his last days happy. I've got my head full of new electric notions, and I want to go to France and experiment. You tell him the whole story; he will be glad to get hold of the planter, and I shall be glad to let it go. I meant to go roving this summer. I'll let it all drop. We have had a run of luck, and luck is apt to turn. We're young yet, you know, J. Benedict Brown, so I put this business into your hands. You're lawyer for the firm."

Brown turned away mournfully; he was convinced more entirely than ever before of the erratic nature of his partner: yesterday with his whole soul bent on furthering the success of the planter; today ready to throw it aside, and to wander away and spend all the money he had earned. Brown mentally resolved that it really was not safe to risk his good name any longer in such keeping, but that he should insist upon being made trustee of a share of his partner's funds, so that Checkley might never come to the ground again.

Checkley called him back in great excitement, when he was leaving the office, a little later. "Look here," said he. "I was going to put this picture into our next almanac as your portrait. I was in the patent-medicine business once, and this was old Dr. Parkins, who made the Spring Bitters. I was going to start him again as John B. Brown, the Pennsylvania farmer and inventor."

"I think it would have been beneath our dignity," responded Brown, severely. "What became of your patent-medicine business? I never heard of that."

"Because it fell through," said Old Shekels, cheerfully. "This was the only thing that never did. You're spoiling a first-class business man for a doubtful lawyer." But Brown laughed, and straightened himself proudly as he went toward Broadway and his other office, which bore the shining brass door-plate with his honored name of J. Benedict Brown.

That evening he confessed all to his wife. It was a great shock, but she bore it bravely. She knew little about business, but she believed with all her heart in respecting the traditions of one's family. Though, after all, one Brown had kindly made money for the other.

THE END

OTHER FICTION TITLES FROM SOLIS PRESS

The King's Jockey – Lesley Gray
(*paperback and ebook*)

The Suffragette Derby of 1913: a woman sacrifices her life for her cause, but what of the man who feels responsible for killing her?

This novel was inspired by the life of royal jockey Herbert 'Bertie' Jones, his rise to fame, his tragic collision with Emily Wilding Davison 100 years ago, and the dramatic events that followed.

The Wreck of the "Grosvenor" – William Clark Russell
(*paperback and ebook*)

This is perhaps Clark Russell's most famous book. It has been described by John Sutherland, Emeritus Professor of Modern English Literature at University College London as: "the most popular mid-Victorian melodrama of adventure and heroism at sea".

List, Ye Landsmen! – William Clark Russell
(*paperback and ebook*)

This book was written at the height of Clark Russell's popularity and according to Dr Andrew Nash, University of Reading: "[Clark Russell] received his largest single payment when Cassell [the publishing company] agreed to pay £1000 for the copyright … around £50,000 in today's money". This seafaring adventure is set in the year of 1815, when Europe was at war, tensions were high and the open seas were a dangerous cauldron of deceit, greed and the forces of nature.

Focus on Sherlock Holmes series – Arthur Conan Doyle
with annotations and notes by George Cavendish
(*ebook exclusive*)

The *Focus on Sherlock Holmes* series introduces the 24 short stories that were published in *The Strand Magazine* between 1891 and 1893.

The ebooks feature notes, annotations and commentary by George Cavendish. We have been faithful to the original editions by including high-quality versions of the original Sidney Paget drawings that accompanied Arthur Conan Doyle's text. Each book features a map of the main locations featured in the story.

See solispress.com for more information and updates